Finder's Magic

BY
C. M. Fleming

The ancients believed
that written words held magic.
So that's why we call it
"spelling."

C.M. Fleming

Connie

Finder's Magic

Finder's Magic

Published by OnStage Publishing
190 Lime Quarry Road, Suite 106J
Madison, AL 35758

Visit us on the web at www.onstagepublishing.com

Copyright 2008 by C. M. Fleming
Front cover by Tom Varnon
Inside illustration by C. M. Fleming
Book layout by ChromeAddict

0-9790857-1-3 Paperback
978-0-9790857-1-0
Printed in the United States of America

For Aubrey, Daniel, Mitchell
and
"The Dude"
who love a good story.

Finder's Magic

Finder's Magic

Chapter One

Wednesday, December 20, 1911

Now I try to abide by the rules same as the next kid, but sometimes you just gotta break one, 'specially if it's an ignorant one. I needed a place to think. That's how I come to be down by the switch-line, a place the mill keeps off limits to the likes of me. I scooted up on a stack of railroad ties and got a splinter in my backside. It'd been a real bad day and it seemed like it was getting worse. That morning, my best friend told me they was trying to make it agin the law for young'uns like me to work the mill.

Then he told me how he planned to leave real soon. Bein' sixteen, more than four years older'n me, he didn't have to worry about bein' put out of a job. He said he'd be coming into a pile of money directly. He wouldn't tell me no more. Even though I knew I shouldn't leave my mama, I still begged Jeb to take me with him. But now, here it was, less than a week from Christmas, and less than two weeks to my twelfth birthday and nothing looked like it was gonna turn out alright. Even my papa was dead an' gone... all because of me. Now, I might not have no job, and my only friend was leavin'.

Finder's Magic

All I had ever wanted to do was raise English Thoroughbred horses with my papa. Might as well hang a big ol' sign around my neck that said, "Hank McCord – World's Biggest Flummox."

So I sat there waiting for the 5:15, a sleek passenger train, to come through, hoping it would make me feel better. The way that train would zip along the tracks behind the mill was a thing of beauty. I liked to imagine where all the people was going-- out west to big cattle ranches, maybe to the Rocky Mountains, or even all the way to California to dig for gold. All the while, I'd be wishing it was taking me far away from Atlanta... and Murphy's Cotton Mill.

At 5:15, folks would be in the dining car, bright as daylight, eating fancy food on clean tablecloths. Sitting in evening shadows, I'd be able to see 'em real good. Colored men in white jackets balanced loaded trays with one hand, going from table to table, serving those folks... them with plenty of money and no cares.

I wondered how in the world those porters could do that with the train moving down the tracks lickety-split. Maybe them that spilled stuff got fired, or worse. I'd ask Jeb about that. He knew most everything. But thinking about all that fancy food made me hungry. I looked in my lunch bucket. Wasn't nothing left but an old, cold biscuit.

That's when I heard 'em--angry voices spoiling for a fight on the other side of the boxcars parked on the switch-line.

I shuddered at the venom in the man's voice. "Nobody blackmails Tugg Arnold and gets away with it." Then I heard a thud followed by a low grunt. It made my stomach hurt just to hear it.

Tugg Arnold was a floor supervisor at the mill where me and Mama worked. Anywhere Tugg showed up, you could be sure Jack Little wasn't far behind. He was Tugg's "assistant." Mostly, they was both just bullies. Thick in the middle, Tugg stood over six foot tall, with wavy, reddish blond hair and a face that always looked sunburned. Jack was even taller, but skinny as a fence post, with stringy dark brown hair, and skin the color

8

of dried corn husks.

"Yeah, nobody!" Jack's shrill voice set my teeth on edge. I winced at the thump of another blow. They was giving somebody the devil.

"Who else knows about our operation?" Tugg bellowed. "Is that what you was schemin' about with that McCord boy this morning?"

My heart skipped a beat at the mention of my name. I tried to think who I'd talked to that morning. I could only think of one person.

"Naw, Mister Arnold. Hank don't know nothin' about it." I would'a known that voice anywhere, though I'd never heard it so weak and shaky. It belonged to my best friend, Jeb Smith.

What had Jeb gone an' done to make them so all-fired mad at him? An' why in the world would Tugg think I had anything to do with whatever it was? My teeth chattered. The wind felt like it was blowing straight off ice. It bit through my raggedy coat as easily as if I didn't even have one on. I stuck my hands under my armpits to stop them from shaking. Jeb hadn't said nothing to me about Tugg or Jack.

If those two caught me there, I didn't have no doubt they'd beat up on me too. They'd see me first thing, too, if they come out from behind the boxcar. I needed to hide 'til I could figure out how to help my friend. Out in the open like that, I was a sitting duck. The only hiding place I could see was inside one of the empty boxcars, but that meant going even closer to the fight. Quiet as I could, I eased off the stack of railroad ties and snuck over to the open door of the car closest to me. When I put my palms on the edge to jump in, a pair of old scuffed brogans blocked my way. I jerked my hands back like I'd been scalded.

Standing there in them worn-out shoes was a colored boy who looked about my age. The gaslight glinted off his black eyes, scowling down at me. He motioned with a hand dark as charcoal and whispered, "Go 'way boy. Find your own hidin' place. They's no room for you in here."

He looked wiry and tough, but I reckoned I had a better

Finder's Magic

chance against a kid my own size than against Tugg and Jack. I puffed out my chest and glared up at him.

"Who you think you're callin' 'boy'?" I whispered. "Back up! Ain't no place else, and they's plenty of room in there."

With a little hop, I pulled myself over the edge of the doorway and stood up. I prayed Tugg and Jack hadn't heard us over all the racket they was raising.

Quick as a snake, the boy's hand snapped out and snatched me into the shadows. "Stay outta sight, then. And keep quiet," he cautioned.

I wrenched away from him. As my eyes got used to the dark of the boxcar, I noticed little slivers of light shining through cracks between the boards. I crept across the floor and peeked out. From the looks of Jeb's face they'd already worked him over pretty bad. Watching what they was doing to Jeb made me sick, almost as much as the shame of being too cowardly to help my friend. I tried to think what to do.

Jeb broke away and started to run. Jack stopped him with an ax handle across his middle. Jeb doubled over and crumpled to the ground. He gave a couple of gurgled coughs and blood trickled from the corner of his mouth. Then he lay still. His open eyes stared straight ahead. I couldn't breathe, standing there looking at my friend's battered body on the ground.

Tugg squatted down and laid his hand on Jeb's chest. He stood up and yanked the ax handle from Jack's hand. "You idiot! You must'a busted a rib into his lungs. He's dead."

My legs nearly buckled. I'd waited too long. Jeb couldn't be dead! Tears filled my eyes 'til I could hardly see. I blinked them away, not knowing what to do, but still glued to the crack in the boxcar.

Jack stuffed his hands in his pockets, and poked his bottom lip out. "Well shoot, Tugg. He was fixin' to get away."

Tugg shook the ax handle in Jack's face like a long finger. "We needed to find out who else he told." He wadded a piece of paper up and stuck it in his pocket. "And take care of 'em." He smacked the ax handle in his other palm.

I tried to swallow, but my spit had all dried up.

"What are we gonna do about this?" Jack pointed his chin at Jeb's body, crumpled on the ground.

"What do you think, genius?" Tugg flung the handle on the ground. "We're gonna make it look like an accident. Then we'll let the sheriff handle it from there." He grinned at Jack.

Jack pushed his hat back and scratched his head. "How you figure on doing that?"

I had to do something. I couldn't let them get away with murder even if it was the last thing I did. Sweat popped out on my forehead. It come to mind that it just might be the last thing I did. What did Tugg mean, "Let the sheriff handle it"? What did the sheriff have to do with Tugg and Jack?

Tugg's booming voice jerked me back. "Look, everyone knows what a drunk Smith's old man was." He checked his pocket watch. "The westbound will be coming along any minute. We'll carry his body over to the other tracks." Tugg pulled a silver flask from the hip pocket of his overalls and unscrewed the cap. He turned it up and took a swig, then cleared his throat. "We'll pour some of this whiskey on him. It'll look like he got drunk and passed out on the tracks." After another swig, Tugg said, "It's getting dark, so the engineer probably won't even see him. Fast as that one goes, wouldn't matter if he did. He couldn't stop."

Jack grinned like a garbage-eatin' possum. "It's a cryin' shame to waste good sippin' whiskey like that." He reached for the flask, but Tugg held it out of his reach. "Aw, come on now, Tugg," Jack whined. "Just one little sip."

Tugg handed the flask to Jack, and said, "See to it you save enough to pour over the body."

Jack's head bobbed up and down a couple of times before Tugg snatched the flask away from him and screwed the cap back on. Jack wiped his chin on his sleeve. Tugg slipped his hands under Jeb's arms. "Don't just stand there. Get his feet."

They laid Jeb's body crosswise on the tracks, on his side, like he was asleep. Tugg pulled the flask out again and emptied it

Finder's Magic

over Jeb.

The wind carried the smell of the whiskey into the boxcar. My stomach heaved. Jeb wasn't no drunk. Nobody would believe that lie. Hot tears streamed down my cheeks. I'd nearly forgotten about the other boy. I glanced over at him. He looked about as sick as I felt.

"They've killed my friend Jeb," I whispered. "I got to do something. I'm going for the sheriff."

He grabbed my arm. "Don't be a fool. Didn't you hear 'em? The sheriff be as big a crook as anybody. You better keep still 'til they leave. Your friend's dead. Ain't nothing you can do now, 'cept get yourself killed, and me too, if they catch us watching."

My legs felt weaker'n a new-born colt's. I had to think. Making my way across the dark floor to a pile of gunny sacks and garbage in the corner, I plopped down.

All of a sudden, that pile of garbage come to life, cussing and slinging his arms. "Get off'n me! This is my place. I was here first." A dirty hobo screamed the words and his spit sprayed in my face. The whites of his eyes flashed in the dark. They was wild as a mad dog's, his breath worse. He grabbed me around the neck. His hands was like a vise grip. My eyes felt as if they was about to pop from their sockets. I clawed at his hands and tried to gasp for air. My head spun.

I heard a loud "thwack," like when Mama's beating the dirt out of a rug. The vise grip on my neck fell away. *Good-lord-in-the-morning!* I'd never take breathing for granted again.

The hobo hugged his arm to his chest. "My arm! You done broke my arm!" He drew back into the corner, whimpering like a whipped dog.

Outside, Tugg yelled, "Who's there?"

The boy threw the pipe down. I'd dropped to my hands and knees, still gasping. He jerked me to my feet. "Come on. We better git!"

I stumbled to the door. The boy jumped to the ground and I followed him. I hit the ground running, just as Jack come busting around the corner.

Tugg come huffing up behind him. "Catch 'em Jack! It's the McCord brat. I knew he was in on it."

I ran like I'd never run before. My hat flew off, but I kept going. I could move pretty fast, but I couldn't keep up with that other boy.

Cinders crunched behind me. I looked over my shoulder. Jack was barely more than an arm's reach from me. In the distance, I seen Tugg dragging the hobo from the boxcar. When I looked ahead, a pile of crates blocked my path. I leaped high as I could, but I stumbled. By the time I got my feet back under me, I felt Jack's hand on my shoulder. He'd a had me for sure, if his foot hadn't got tangled in one of the crates. He lost his grip on me and tumbled headlong into the stack. That gave me a chance to put some distance between me an' him. I could hear Jack kicking at the crates and cussing a blue streak.

I left the railroad and raced into the trashy, overgrown back lot of the mill. The other boy ducked between some buildings some fifty feet ahead. When I made the turn, I stopped dead in my tracks. He was gone, just plain vanished.

Then I noticed dead weeds mashed down and some loose boards at the bottom of one of the shacks. I bent down and peered into the darkness. The weeds nearly hid the opening to the crawl-space under the floor. It had the musky smell of rats but there wasn't no time for nothing else. Tugg and Jack was too close behind. When I heard Tugg yell, I shoved the boards aside and slid under the shack, feet first.

The second I cleared the opening, a hand clamped over my mouth. I tried to yell, but then he hissed, "Shhh."

I'd accidentally found the same hiding place as him...again. He let go and put a finger to his lips. I nodded and pushed the weeds up as best I could. We hurried to prop the loose boards back in place. When my eyes got used to the dark, I looked around for signs of rats. Mercy, I hated rats. Inside the crawl-space, their smell was even stronger. The only thing I hated worse was snakes. They liked the same hiding places, too. With

Finder's Magic

it being winter though, there wasn't much danger of coming across a snake.

We'd barely got the boards in place when we heard Jack's pounding footsteps and ragged breathing. He stopped in the weeds, smack in front of us, trampling out any sign we might'a left. He leaned over and put his hands on his knees, gasping for breath. He was standing so close, I could see blood-splatters on his blue work shirt. The specks of blood looked black in the twilight. Tugg hollered in the distance.

When Tugg caught up, he sounded more out of breath than Jack. Sweat poured from his red face. He had my hat wadded up in his fist. "Where'd...they...go?" The air wheezed in and out through his mouth. He pulled a bandana from his pocket to mop his face. A piece of wadded up paper fell out on the ground.

"Dunno," Jack said, panting. "They just up an' disappeared."

Tugg swore and smacked the wall. It startled me so that I bumped my head on the boards above me.

"What was that?" Jack whispered.

I held my breath 'til thought I would pass out.

"I didn't hear nothing," Tugg said, still wheezing. "What'd it sound like?"

The boy glared at me. I glared back at him and rubbed my aching head.

"Sounded like something fell inside." Jack's feet come closer, and then he stood on tiptoes. I guessed he was looking in the window. "I don't see nothing. Probably a rat or something." He stepped back. "You reckon Smith told the McCord kid about our operation?" Jack asked.

There was that word again, "operation."

"Sure, they had to be in on it together," Tugg said.

In on what? Jeb never told me nothing about Tugg or Jack, nor no "operation" neither.

Tugg went on. "Why else would the McCord kid be hanging around the train yard so late? When I caught 'em lollygaggin' this morning, Smith made up some tale about empty spools."

It wasn't made up. My spools was empty.

Tugg stuffed my hat in the front of his overalls. "The kid could be hidin' in one of these shacks. Let's check 'em out." As they walked away, he said, "Look for a busted window, or broken lock."

We watched them, as best we could, check every weather-beaten building, trying doors and peeping through dingy windows. Pretty soon, they come back and stood in the weeds in front of our hiding place once more.

Tugg bit off a chaw of tobacco and stuffed it into his cheek. "We'll catch up with 'em sooner or later, and when we do..." He punched a fist into his palm.

I looked over at the other boy. His eyes was bottomless black holes.

Jack said, "All right, we know the white one is the McCord brat. We know where to find him, but what about the nigger?"

I could almost feel the colored boy bristle at Jack's insult.

Tugg spit out a stream of tobacco juice. It slithered down the weeds. "I didn't get a good look at his face. There ain't none of them working at the mill." He looked around, and then, in a raised voice said, "McCord! You got any sense at all, you'll keep your lousy little mouth shut... unless you want the same thing Smith got."

Just then, the whistle of the westbound train ripped through the cold evening air. I shuddered. Even though I knew Jeb couldn't feel nothing, the thought of his bones being crushed beneath the train's grinding wheels was more'n I could take. For a split second, I pictured me and that colored boy laid out beside Jeb on those cold steel tracks.

I stuffed my fist in my mouth and swallowed my sobs. *I sure didn't want what Jeb got.*

Jack kicked a dirt clod. It busted on the boards in front of us, and pieces of dirt shot through into my face. "I'd a caught the little brat if he hadn't thrown a crate under my feet."

Tugg snorted. "Hell, you'd stumble over your own two big

feet just walking down the street. Let's go. We got to make sure the brat didn't manage to slip past us. You go let that drunk of a sheriff know what happened, so he can keep a look out for him, too. We can't take a chance on lettin' the kid get to the boss man."

We could hear them grumbling and arguing as they left.

Sweat trickled down my sides. Whatever Tugg and Jack was up to, the sheriff seemed to be in on it. I was in deep trouble. We lay there for what seemed a long time in the crawl-space, staring out through the cracks, but not looking at each other.

"You think they'll come back?" I whispered.

"How should I know what they'll do?" he asked. "They your people."

"They ain't *my* people," I snapped. "Tugg, the big one, he's my *boss*." Finally, I couldn't take it no longer. I had to get out. I knocked the boards away and shot out. Leaning back against the rough, warped wood of the shack, I took a deep breath and tried to decide how I could slip past Tugg and Jack and get home to Mama.

The colored boy crawled out, too, his eyes darting this way and that. He leaned against the wall beside me. "What you gonna do, now? They knows you. They gonna be lookin' for you."

I brushed some cobwebs from my pants, and crossed my arms over my chest, cold again. "I don't know. I got to find some way to get to Mister Murphy. He's the man what owns the mill. Ain't no way I can go back there tonight, though. They'll be watching for me at home, too. Dang it, I can't just run off. Mama's depending on me, 'specially since Papa died."

"Well, you ain't gonna help her none if you dead. What'd y'all do to make 'em so mad?"

"I ain't done nothing, blast it! I don't even know what Jeb did, but it ain't right for them to get away with killing him. He's my best friend." I stopped. "Jeb was my best friend."

He looked at me. "I know how bad you feel 'bout that, but you can't bring him back."

Finder's Magic

How could he know how I felt? "Jeb weren't the kind to blackmail nobody. He must've found out something real bad about them. I ain't got no idea what it was. And from what they said, it wouldn't do no good to go to the sheriff." For a second I wondered if maybe they just made up the part about the sheriff. "Well, maybe if I could get to him first, he might listen to me. I've got half a mind to try."

"You got that right," he said.

"Huh? Got what right?" I asked, digging a piece of dirt out of the corner of my eye.

"That part about havin' half a mind. That's all you got, if you think the sheriff gonna listen to you. It's your word agin theirs. The sheriff ain't gonna listen to no wet-behind-the-ears young'un. Besides, I know him. He be the biggest crook of all. He'll throw you so far back in jail you ain't never gonna see the light of day no more. Or worse." He made like he was yanking a rope up around his neck.

I balled up my fists. I wanted to hit something. "It was murder, plain and simple. You seen it, same as me. He'd have to listen to us."

He held up his hands as if to push me away. "Whoa, now. You wanna go get yourself killed, that be your business. You do whatever you gotta do, but I ain't gonna have no part in going to no white lawman. You never seen me, an' I never seen you. You got that straight?"

I kicked the boards at the bottom of the shack with my heel. "They ain't gonna stop with killing Jeb. They're after me now, 'cause they think I know something. I don't know what I'm gonna do. I ain't got no place to go." My teeth chattered. I bit my lip to keep from bawling and wiped my nose on my sleeve. "Me an' Mama ain't done nothing to deserve this."

I looked down and saw the wadded up paper that Tugg had dropped. I picked it up and smoothed it out a little. There wasn't nothing on it but some names and numbers.

"What's that?" the boy asked.

"Nothing, just something that fell outta Tugg's pocket." I

wadded it up and started to throw it away, but then for some reason, I shoved it into my pocket.

He stared at me for awhile, as if he was trying to make up his mind about something. Then he said, "I sure nuf know what it's like not to have nobody, nor no place to go." He grabbed my elbow and said, "I can't believe I'm sayin' this, but I knows a safe place you can hide out, at least 'til you can figure out what to do."

We snuck away from the mill, toward the river and the railroad tracks, staying in the shadows. A smirk settled over his face. "So, you that McCord *brat*," he said. "My name's Calvin Yates."

I didn't appreciate the smirk, or his smart mouth, but I said, "My name's Henry McCord. *Most* folks call me Hank."

We both jumped when a screech owl shrieked from a clump of trees close by. "Let's get outta here." Calvin took off running, and I lit out, too... right on his heels.

Chapter Two

Calvin led me down under the railroad trestle through shoulder-high ragweed, black and slimy from the freeze. By now it was getting pretty dark. A ghostly mist rose from the river. I heard a clanking sound overhead. Twenty foot above the Peachtree River some sort of big metal bucket dangled on a rusty cable off to one side of the railroad bridge. I couldn't believe it when Calvin climbed the rickety wooden ladder and stepped into the bucket.

"Climb up," he said. "We got to git across the river. This be the best way."

"What's that contraption? It don't look like it'll hold one person, let alone the both of us," I said. "Maybe I can find a shallow place and wade across, or just run across the bridge."

Calvin shook his head. "The railroad workers used this to carry tools and such back and forth when they was building bridge. It may be old, but it's strong. You some kind of fraidy cat, or just a dang fool? They's sinkholes all over this river." He waved his hand toward the river. "Suit yourself, though. You could get caught out on the bridge. Or you could drown. You could freeze--or you could get your scrawny, white *be*-hind in this bucket, afore I change my mind 'bout helpin' you."

Finder's Magic

"Hold on," I said. I didn't cotton to being bossed around by some uppity Negro. Even so, I climbed the ladder, got into the bucket and squatted down...gripping the sides so hard my knuckles turned white. The two of us hardly fit.

Calvin said, "Don't look down."

Too late! My eyes focused on the muddy river a long way below. Little dots of light winked here and there on the surface while the dark water whispered threats as it tumbled downstream.

Calvin stood, his back to me. He took hold of the rusty cable overhead and strained against it. The pulley screeched, but the bucket only moved a few inches.

"You ever done this before?" My voice cracked.

Calvin tried once more with no better luck. He looked over his shoulder at me. "Look, I said I'd help you, but I ain't nobody's slave. I can't do this all my myself. We be too heavy. Now get up and help me."

I wasn't sure my legs would support me, but I stood and, with sweaty palms, gripped the cable. My head spun when I peeked over the side. I pulled as hard as I could, but my hands slipped. The bucket lurched to one side and I just about took a header over the side. The cable creaked and groaned.

"Lord, help me! I ain't gonna live through this night." I hoped my prayer would save me.

"You gonna get us drowned!" Calvin snapped.

"I dropped to my knees. "Me? You're the one got us up here."

When the bucket finally stopped pitching and bucking, Calvin eased around to face me. Flakes of rust sprinkled down on us like pepper.

Through clenched teeth, his words slow, he said, "Look. Stand up real slow and easy like, with your feet apart. Like mine. To do this, we gots to pull together."

I locked eyes with him and stood, wiping my clammy hands on my pants. Calvin turned forward, careful so's not to tip the bucket. His hands shook when he reached up for the cable. We

Finder's Magic

pulled together and the bucket moved several inches. "That's it. First right, now left," he said.

I stuck my tongue out at the back of his head, but I gritted my teeth and concentrated on matching him pull for pull. Before I knew it, the bucket clanked to a stop on the other side of the river. Calvin stepped out onto a little wooden platform and held the bucket steady. I stared back across the river. My heart pounded and my hands burned from pullin' on the rusty cable. I don't know how, but we'd beat death twice in one night.

We walked through a cluster of shanties along the river bank to a trail that snaked into the woods. Lamp lights flickered through the shanty windows. The smell of sizzling pork was pure heaven. It reminded me of better times back on the farm. My mouth watered. At the end of the short trail, a run-down cabin stood off to itself. Lazy smoke twirled from a sooty, rusted smokestack in the tattered tarpaper roof. Soft drumbeats kept time with a woman's singing. I couldn't make out any of the words, but the tune was the most sorrowful sound I'd ever heard.

"This your house?" I asked.

Calvin shook his head. He put his finger to his lips and whispered, "This be the Finder's house. I stay with her sometimes." He tilted his head to one side, listening to the mournful song coming from inside. He pointed to the rickety front steps and said, "Wait here. Everybody says she be a witch. She's prob'ly conjurin' up a spell against a bad sickness or evil." He looked at me over his shoulder and grinned.

"Wait," I whispered. "Who's the Finder?" *Or what is she?* I wanted to ask, but didn't. The words "conjurin'", "spell" and "evil" made the hair on the back of my neck stand up. "Besides," I whispered, "don't we need a hider, instead of a finder? Why can't we go stay with your mama and papa?"

Calvin scowled and pointed to the steps. "Sit!"

I'd a run, but I didn't know where to go, so I sat on the steps, as Mama would say, like an ol' settin' hen.

Calvin tiptoed to the door and turned to put his ear against

Finder's Magic

it, right as it opened. The oldest, blackest woman I'd ever seen towered in the doorway. She held her head high, her back straight as a board. She was dressed in white from head to toe. Puffs of crinkly snow-white hair sprung from the scarf on her head. Her clothes was so bright she almost looked like she was lit from the inside by lightnin' bugs.

Looking straight ahead, she asked, "Yes, then, 'oo is it?"

She didn't sound at all like Calvin. Come to think of it, she didn't sound a bit like anyone from around here. She sounded more like them fancy-dressed English folk who had visited the mill once.

Calvin wasn't no more than a foot from her. I wondered why she acted as if she didn't know him, or even see him. *Lord help us, we'd come to a crazy woman's house.*

Calvin cleared his throat and said, "It's me, Miz Mancala, Calvin."

The steps creaked when I stood. She turned her face toward me. Her pale eyes told the story. She wouldn't see nothing out of them blind eyes.

"I'd begun to think you'd found other accommodations for the night," she said. "And who've you brought along, luv?" she asked, sounding for all the world like some high and mighty queen. At least, I reckoned that's how a queen would sound.

"This be Hank McCord, Miz Mancala." Calvin looked around at me and motioned with his hand as if I should say something.

I closed my gaping mouth. "I, ah--how do, ma'am," I finally managed to croak.

The old lady stepped back out of the doorway and said, "Well, don't just stand out in the bloomin' cold. Come in, gentlemen, do come in."

I swear she motioned us to come in like we was dukes ourselves or something. Calvin jerked his head for me to follow. My jaw had kinda slipped back down. I shut my mouth, hitched up my patched britches, and followed them into the dark shanty. My knees knocked so hard, they must have sounded like Papa

Finder's Magic

playing the spoons, but all I could hear was the pounding of my heart.

Chapter Three

A tea kettle on a potbellied stove rattled and hissed. Strange medicine smells, bad as the liniment Papa used on the horses, floated in the air--smells of secret potions for Lord only knows what. Calvin lit a lantern, shucked off his coat and hung it on a nail by the door. I didn't see no shrunken heads swinging from the rafters, just bunches of dried plants and flowers.

She's probably got the real witchy stuff hid away.

The old woman went to the stove and moved the kettle off to the side. "I was about to have a spot of tea and some nice little biscuits. Would you care to join me?"

I knew it! Just like the Queen of England!

Calvin answered for the both of us. "Yessum, if you please." I frowned at him and shook my head, but he didn't pay me no mind.

Miz Mancala moved about smooth as a swan on a lake. If I hadn't seen her eyes, I wouldn't never believed she couldn't see. She poured hot water into a fancy china teapot sitting next to some dainty teacups. Then she put some kind of little cookies on a plate, set it all on a tray and carried it to us. Calvin took the tray from her and set it on the floor. I wondered why he didn't put the tray on the tiny table beside the old beat-up rocking chair, 'til I looked closer. It weren't no table at all, but some kind of drum. It must a been the one I heard from outside.

Miz Mancala sat down in the rocking chair. "Would you be so kind as to pour, Calvin?"

Calvin poured the first cup, added some cream then handed the cup and saucer to Miz Mancala.

The old lady breathed in the steam. "Ahh, splendid." She cocked her head to one side. "Please, sit down lads. Make yourselves comfortable."

By now I had come down with a permanent case of drop-jaw. Calvin gave my arm a yank. We sat cross-legged on a worn braided rug at Miz Mancala's feet. The fire in the stove crackled, chasing away some of the chill from my bones. I shrugged off my jacket and laid it across my lap.

Calvin poured me a cup of steaming tea from the teapot. I'd never seen anything so fancy as that teapot. I wondered where the old lady had got something so fine. The pot had pink roses painted all around. They looked like the wild roses, Mama's favorites, that grew back home along the fences. The teacups and saucers had the same roses. Them fancy things sure didn't look like they belonged in Miz Mancala's run-down cabin.

Calvin picked up the plate of cookies and held it out to me. Miz Mancala'd called 'em "biscuits." That ain't what biscuits look like where I come from. I worried about what might be baked inside--toad's tongue, lizard's legs, or flies' wings? At first, I held back from taking one, but my stomach growled like a hungry dog guardin' a bone.

Calvin grinned and bit into a cookie. "Um, umm, umm. Mighty fine." A few crumbs fell on his pants' leg. He licked the tip of his finger, touched it to the crumbs to pick them up, then stuck it in his mouth. His eyes danced with devilment.

I tried a sip of the tea, but it was bitter and burned my tongue. The cookies looked all right. *How much could a little baked lizard's leg hurt a body, anyhow?* I picked one up. They smelled good enough. When I nibbled the edge, the sweet taste of molasses and cinnamon spread over my tongue. I gobbled the rest of it in one bite and eyed the rest of the plate.

Miz Mancala said, "Go on, help yourselves to the lovely little biscuits," as if she'd read my mind. "Dear Elizabeth brings me something quite delightful most days, since I helped her find her favorite rolling pin." A peculiar smile come across her face, like someone who's got a secret joke.

I didn't know Miz Elizabeth, but she sure could bake molasses cookies. When I reached for another cookie, something tickled the back of my other arm. It felt like a spider crawling up. I dropped the cookie and brushed my arm to knock it away. My hand bumped a furry head instead. I spun around. A big yellow cat sniffed my hand. His whiskers, soft as spiders' legs, brushed across my palm. He let out a peculiar sound, a purr, a growl and a meow all rolled up together.

Miz Mancala chuckled and said, "What say you, Mehuru? What do you make of this young lad?"

The cat rubbed his face against my hand, and then curled up in my lap with his chin on my knee. I scratched behind his ears. He closed his eyes and purred so loud it sounded like the Mister Murphy's Model T.

Miz Mancala threw back her head and laughed. "Mehuru is never wrong. He sees into hearts quite the way I see lost things. We are kindred spirits, he and I."

For a time the only sounds was Mehuru's purring and the creaking of Miz Mancala's rocking chair.

I sat there and munched cookies, making sure to keep my lips closed. Not that Miz Mancala could tell, with her being blind and all, but Mama always taught me to mind my manners. I tried to picture Mama sitting down to tea and cookies with a Negra woman like Miz Mancala--Mama tired and covered with lint from the mill and Miz Mancala, old as Methuselah in her spotless white clothes, smiling politely. *Never in a million years!*

Miz Mancala spoke, her words soft and low. "I heard the flutter of a bird's wings against my window this morning. A sure sign of death. That's why you've sought me. Is it not?"

Finder's Magic

I gasped and sucked a piece of cookie sideways down my windpipe. I coughed so hard tears come to my eyes. Calvin whacked me on the back while he answered Miz Mancala's question. "Yessum. We seen it. It was awful."

The cat leaped outta my lap and ran slap into Miz Mancala's chair. She leaned over and picked him up. Draping him over her arm, she stroked his fur, cooing to him. "Poor darling, Mehuru. You mustn't dash around so. You must remember to move more slowly. Let your beautiful whiskers be your eyes."

My scalp prickled. Good-lord-almighty, the cat was blind, too! It gave me a creepy feeling, like I'd touched something dead. Right then I wanted to get out of there and as far away as I could get.

Miz Mancala settled the cat in her lap and turned her face to Calvin. "And the men, are they aware you saw?"

Calvin looked over at me. "Yessum, they knows, but they didn't follow us here. I made sure."

The old woman kept stroking the cat. "No, those white louts are not likely to come here. At least not right away. And most certainly not alone."

"How did you know they was white men? I asked.

"Why else would a white boy come to an old black woman for help? If a colored man had killed someone, you would bloody well go to the white men in charge."

"But how did you know *I'm* white? I, ah, didn't think you could see me."

A witchy cackle rose up from someplace deep inside her. Goose-flesh popped up on my arms. She said. "There are more ways to see than with eyes, lad. No need to be afraid. It's really no mystery. Since my sight left me, I tend to pay closer attention to my other senses." She ticked off the reasons on her fingers. "First, your speech gives you away. Secondly, you have the smell of the mill about you, and third, none of our people work at the mill."

She knew someone had got killed and I was a white boy working at the mill. That really spooked me, 'cause no one had told her none of it. I sniffed my jacket. I couldn't smell nothing.

Calvin spoke up again. "It was them overseers at the mill, Miz Mancala. They beat up a friend of Hank's, and then ditched his body on the train track. They seen us, and chased us!" He took a deep breath. "They knows Hank. They be lookin' for him. He ain't got no pa to help him. What should he do, Miz Mancala?"

The old woman kept on rocking, brushing the cat's shiny coat. I wondered how some old blind witch-woman with an English accent could help me.

"Hank," she said, "people call me 'The Finder.' Do you know why?"

"No, ma'am." I wasn't one to chew my nails, but I bit my thumbnail into the quick. It stung and the blood tasted salty on my tongue. I figured she was fixin' to tell me, whether I wanted to know or not.

"When people lose things they seek help from me. Most often, they already know where the missing item is." She waved her hand as if shooing a fly. "Only in their minds is it hidden. I help them look with their third eye..." she put one long finger to the middle of her forehead, "...or their mind's eye." The old lady stopped for a sip of tea.

Their third eye? Now that was just plain creepy. I stole a quick glance at Calvin. He took another sip of tea, too. The old woman's rambling didn't seem to bother him. Guess he'd heard it all before.

Miz Mancala went on talking. "With a bit of my help, they are able to find the lost item. Sometimes, however, the thing missing is the truth. That is always more difficult to find."

"Excuse me ma'am, but how can the truth be hard to find? Don't everyone know the truth?" I couldn't hardly sit still. It felt like bugs was crawling all over my skin. *Did she know what Jeb knew about Tugg and Jack? Did she know my own dark secret about Papa?*

"Perhaps," she said.

29

Finder's Magic

I wondered which questions she was answering--the one I asked out loud, or the ones in my head.

"One person's truth is not the same as another's," she said. "Often times the journey to truth is painful. That journey may be filled with sorrow, danger and fear."

All this talk was getting me nowhere. If she knew, why'd she keep talking in riddles? I don't got time for riddles. My best friend's body lay dead and mangled on the railroad tracks. Now his murderers was after me, and Mama couldn't get by without me. Even if we managed to get away from Tugg and Jack, how would we live without our jobs at the mill? We didn't even have the farm to go back to. I stood and said, "Miz Mancala, I think I better just go home. My mama will know what to do."

Calvin jumped up. "And when those killers catch you, what you gonna do? They gonna make you tell where I am. I was crazy for bringin' you here!"

"You think I'm some kind of yellow-bellied coward that would do such a thing as that?" I balled up my fists. "I ain't that kind. I work an honest job and I keep my word!"

Calvin stuck out his chin. "You sure didn't do nothin' for your *best* friend."

I spun around to face him. "There wasn't nothing I *could* do. You said so yourself. You even told me not to go to the sheriff. *You're* the coward."

He poked his finger in my chest. "You're just a dumb cracker."

Then I yelled the meanest thing I could think of. "Nigger!" I swung a hay-maker at him but he dodged it. He bent at the waist and rammed me in the gut with his head. We went to the floor rolling, kicking, swinging and gouging.

Next thing I knew we was both gasping for air and soaked to the skin with cold water. Miz Mancala stood over us with an empty water pail. Her fancy teapot lay shattered on the floor.

Miz Mancala scowled down at us. "No good comes from name calling. There will be no more of it. Do you lads understand me?"

"Yessum," we answered together, but the look in Calvin's eyes said it weren't settled.

"Good." She tossed a pile of rags on the floor and said, "Now dry the floor." She sat down in her rocking chair. "Like it or not, the two of you shall have to work together."

Calvin spied the broken teapot. "Oh no, Miz Mancala, we broke the teapot your husband give you." He picked up the pieces, real gentle like, and held them in his cupped hands. "I'm sorry Miz Mancala."

The old lady's mouth dropped open like she was gonna cry, but no sounds came out. She turned away. "No matter." Her voice quivered. "I still have the memory of its beauty."

We sopped up the water off the floor, wringing the rags out into the bucket she'd emptied on us. Calvin spread the rags out on the wood box to dry. "You want me to go fetch another bucket of water from the spring?" he asked, his teeth chattering.

"It can wait until morning. You'll catch your death in those wet clothes," Miz Mancala said. "Get quilts from the trunk and hang your clothes by the stove to dry."

I stripped down to my drawers and socks, but that was as far as I was going. My socks was more hole that cotton. I tucked my feet under the quilt and stole a look at Calvin. He didn't have no socks on. The bottoms of his feet was real light colored compared to the rest of him. He caught me staring, pulled his knees up and covered his feet. There we sat on opposite sides of the hot stove wrapped in quilts that smelt like cedar.

The blind yeller cat rubbed against Miz Mancala's shins. She reached down and scooped him up into her lap. "Now that you have that out of the way, let's see if we can decide what you must do." She cocked her head, as if listening for one of us to argue.

She turned her face toward me. "I agree with Calvin that it would not be a good idea for you to return to your home tonight, Hank. But your mum will be worried. We must get word to her. Tomorrow we will send someone."

At the same time, Calvin and me asked, "Who?"

She held up her long bony hand. "Hank, where is your mum, now?"

"My mama? I reckon she's still at the mill."

Calvin's eyes opened wide. "What your mama be doin' there so late?"

"She's workin' a double today. Mister Murphy moved her up to weaver after my papa passed. It pays more. He let me start working on the line at the mill, too. I reckon he felt it was the least he could do, seeing it was working at his old mill that killed Papa." I stole a quick glance at Miz Mancala to see if she caught my lie about Papa's death.

Miz Mancala tapped her finger to her cheek. "The men would not be watching for a young girl, perhaps one selling eggs."

Calvin scratched his head. "I reckon not, but they ain't no girls here, 'cept you, Miz Mancala.

I thought the same thing. I didn't figure Miz Mancala could find her way to our cabin with her being blind and all. She'd said, "young girl." That for sure left her out. Besides, it would take a mighty brave girl to run the risk of facing up to Tugg and Jack. I don't think I ever met one that brave. Shoot, I didn't even know any boys that brave. Mama would'a probably stood up to them, though. She's always been pretty spunky, 'specially when it come to looking out for me.

Miz Mancala didn't answer Calvin's question. Instead, she asked, "How tall have you grown, Calvin?" She set the cat on the floor and stood up from her rocking chair. "Come here." She pointed to the floor in front of her feet.

Calvin stared at the old lady, pure puzzlement on his face. He shrugged. Then hugging the quilt to his body, he padded over to Miz Mancala.

"My, but you are getting tall," she said putting her hands on his shoulders. She moved her hands to his middle and laughed. "Ah, but you're still thin as a pine sapling. I suppose I can pin in the waist of one of my skirts to fit you."

I didn't have no idea what she meant, but Calvin had figured it out. "Oh, no," he said throwing up his hands and almost dropping his quilt. "I ain't fixin' to wear no skirt for nobody. Not even if they offered to pay me a hunnard dollars in pure gold!"

It was the craziest idea I ever heard of. Although, with Calvin standing there wrapped from chin to toe in a quilt, I could picture him in a skirt. I was glad the old woman didn't want me to put on no skirt.

"We shall discuss it in the morning," she said. You will know what you must do. Everything will work out, you'll see."

Miz Mancala might be good at finding lost things, but this was gonna take a whole lot more fixin' than finding somebody's ol' lost rolling pin.

Finder's Magic

Chapter Four

Pitch-black night surrounded the cabin. Miz Mancala sat on a cot next to the wall and unwound the white scarf from her head. Her long crinkly hair tumbled down when she took off the scarf. She turned her head toward Calvin. "Now would be a good time for your reading, Calvin. You know where the reader is." She picked up a comb from a narrow shelf above her bed.

How could she think about reading at a time like this?

My stomach tied up in double knots as I sat there on the floor. I was still cold from the dousing Miz Mancala gave us, but steaming inside because of what Calvin said about me not helping my friend. I had *wanted* to help Jeb. I was gonna help Jeb. I pictured Mama pacing the floor of our cabin, looking out the window for me. Poor Jeb. No one was looking for him. He didn't have nobody to care.

Calvin stalked over to some shelves nailed to the wall. He looked like one of them Indians in a dime western story, wrapped from head to toe in a blanket. All he needed was a band of feathers around his head. I couldn't help but grin. He caught my look and sent one back that said, "You'll be sorry you messed with me."

I shot him just as mean a look right back.

He pulled down a skinny book with a worn cover, then brought the lamp to the floor and sat down beside it. He opened the book, turned a few pages, then snapped it shut. "I don't 'member what page we was on," he mumbled.

"What page we *were* on," Miz Mancala corrected as she pulled the comb through her hair. She rubbed some kind of sweet-smelling oil in her palms, smoothed it over her hair and combed it some more. "You are in the fifth reader, are you not?" she asked.

"Yessum" Calvin answered, his lips all pouty.

"Then I believe the next selection is 'The ABC's on page twelve." She twisted her hair into a long braid.

Calvin opened the book and read.

ABC'S

A – Adorn: He adorns His creation with leaf
and blossom. Kissing it with the sweet morning dew.
Admire His artwork in quiet re-re...

He stumbled over a word. Miz Mancala said, "Reverie. The word is reverie. It means to think deeply about something.

Calvin repeated the word, then went on reading.

B – Blameless: Be blameless in His sight.
Love one another as He has loved you.
Lift your brother from the pit and restore his faith.
C – Courage: Let not your courage fail.
He will fortify you and guide your
steps. He will light your path with wisdom.

Calvin Yates was plumb full of surprises. None of the kids at the mill could read near that good--least of all, me. It stuck in my craw that a colored kid had got more schooling than me. There hadn't been no time for school, or learning the three R's at the mill. But at least I had a job.

Miz Mancala nodded. "Excellent, Calvin. Your reading is

getting stronger each time you read. Good night lads, sleep well." She lay down on the cot and closed her eyes.

Calvin put the book back on the shelf, then set the lamp on the cupboard and blew it out. He stretched out on the floor with his back towards me. I rolled up my jacket for a pillow and curled up on the rug close to the stove. I wasn't looking forward to a night in that spooky little cabin. It was gonna be a long sleepless night.

Before long I could hear Miz Mancala's breathing change to slow deep breaths. She'd fallen asleep. Calvin still had his back to me.

"Psst. Calvin, you asleep?"

Calvin turned over, the glow from the stove shining on his face and dancing in his eyes. "How can a body sleep with you over there hissin' like some ol' snake?" He sat up, propping himself with his elbow. "If you need the outhouse, don't expect me to go along to hold your hand. You on your own."

"Naw! That ain't it. I just wanted to ask you something," I said. "Sorry I bothered you. Go on back to sleep."

"Well, I'm awake, now. What you want?"

"It's just...well, I wondered where you learned to read so good."

Calvin's scowl softened, and he grinned for the first time. "Miz Mancala learned, uh, taught me."

"Humph! How can a blind woman learn someone to read?" I didn't want him to get the big-head, thinkin' I was bragging on him, and I didn't want him to know I was jealous, neither.

"She got every word memorized. Ain't that something?" Calvin shook his head. She used to teach the slaves how to read, even though it was agin the law. She say they's power in the wrote, uh, written word."

Slavery had ended with the Civil War, a long time ago. I could tell Miz Mancala was real old, maybe even close to a hundred. "Well, how'd she learn, if it was again the law?" I asked.

Calvin shrugged. "I think she went to some white mission school in Africa when she was a little girl."

I didn't rightly know what a "mission school" was, or why they'd let a colored person go there, but I had something else on my mind. "Calvin, how come you helped me?"

He snorted. "I been wonderin' the same thing, myself."

"Well, what was you doin' over by the mill anyway?"

"Now see there! That's another reason I should'a left you there. White folks always thinkin' someone like me up to no good."

I sat up. If that was "another reason," I wondered what the first one was. "That ain't what I was sayin'." My voice rose. He sure had a way of riling me up, even when I was trying to be nice.

He scooted closer. "Keep your voice down." He glanced over at Miz Mancala. "You gonna wake her."

She hadn't moved a lick.

"Maybe you didn't say it, but you thought it," he added.

"I didn't think no such of a thing!" I growled. "I just wondered. I go there to watch the evening train come through sometimes...when I need to think about something."

The fire snapped and the wood shifted in the stove, sending sparks out around the loose-fitting door. We both jumped.

Calvin picked up an iron poker propped against the wood box. He opened the stove door with it. "I pick up coal what fall off the train. Not that it's any of your business." He jabbed at the burning wood with the poker. "My daddy told me once it falls off the coal car, it belong to whoever pick it up." He jabbed at the fire again. "He say it's 'salvage'."

"Salvage?" I asked.

"Yeah, that means it ain't stealin' if somebody takes it." Calvin put a log in the fire, closed the door and then propped the poker back against the wood box.

"I never said you was stealin'. Your daddy sounds like a smart man," I said. "Where is he?"

Calvin looked at me hard. "Dead." He went back to his pallet and curled up with his back to me.

"Well, what about your mama?" I asked. When he didn't

Finder's Magic

answer me, I laid down too. In the distance I heard the long warning blast of a train's whistle before it crossed the bridge. Then come the clackity-clack of the wheels on the trestle. As long as I lived, the sounds of a train would remind me of Jeb.

I felt so lonesome I ached.

Chapter Five

Thursday, December 21, 1911

I shot up, my heart pounding when Calvin dumped an armload of wood in the box, inches from my head.

"You gonna sleep all day?" He was already dressed. Miz Mancala shuffled around her little kitchen.

My face burned at getting caught asleep. "Ma'am," I said, ignoring Calvin, "is there anything you want me to do?" Quick as I could, I pulled on my pants and shirt under the quilt. They was stiff, but warm and dry.

Miz Mancala waved her arm in the direction of the bucket on the counter, like she could see it setting there. "We need water. There is a spring behind the house."

The sky was still clouded over. The sun glowed like a big orange persimmon through the clouds. I looked around before leaving the porch. Tugg and Jack was still out there somewhere, looking for me. Following a worn footpath around the house, I found the spring. Clumps of saw grass around it wore a fuzz of white frost and a thin layer of ice glistened on the water. I cracked the ice with the bucket and dipped it into the clear, cold water.

Finder's Magic

When I walked back around to the front porch, Calvin stood there waiting on me. He pointed to a wash basin and said, "You got to wash up before you can eat."

"With this water?" I set the bucket down with a thump. "I had to break the ice to get it."

Calvin smirked. "Miz Mancala's real picky 'bout folks washing."

I poured some of the water in the basin and washed my face and hands. It was so cold it felt like hundreds of needles pricking my skin all at once. Calvin handed me a towel. He picked up the basin and tossed the wash water out onto the ground, set it down and turned to go in.

"Wait a minute," I said. "Ain't you gonna wash up, too?"

"Oh, I washed up already," Calvin said, the smirk growing to a grin. "Inside."

I knew that was a lie. Miz Mancala had emptied the water pail on us the night before. If I hadn't been so durned cold, I'd been burning up. He tricked me into washing in ice cold water for pure orneriness. I stared at the bucket of water sitting on the porch. For minute, I considered throwing the rest of it on Calvin, but then I'd just have to fight him again. I picked up the bucket and carried it inside to Miz Mancala.

We sat by the stove, ate hot biscuits and drank tea. I'd rather had coffee, but the biscuits was good. These was real biscuits, fat and golden, smeared with plenty of butter, not some fancy little muffins or cookies some queen would eat. It took awhile, but I finally got warmed up again.

After breakfast, Miz Mancala went straight to a trunk in the corner and lifted out a bright-colored skirt. She ran her hand over it the same way she petted the cat. She shook her head. "No, not this one. It would draw too much attention."

"How does she do that?" I whispered to Calvin, but he wasn't paying me no mind.

"Touch, my dear." Miz Mancala rubbed her fingertips together. "It is in the touch." She refolded the colorful skirt and laid it back in the trunk. Then she took out a plain-looking gray skirt and blouse. "Ah, yes. These should do quite nicely."

Calvin protested. "Miz Mancala, I ain't gonna do no such of a thing."

With her crinkly white eyebrows arched, Miz Mancala said, "Why Calvin, I assumed you wished to help your chum. It is, of course, entirely up to you." She stood by the trunk holding the clothes, waiting for Calvin's answer.

Calvin looked at me, then back at Miz Mancala. "But I-he-he ain't no 'chum' of mine. I mean, shoot! I felt sorry for him and all, but what's any white person ever done to help me? What if somebody see me? I'd be shamed. They'd laugh me clean outta Georgia." He paced back and forth in front of Miz Mancala. "Let him go on home to his mama if that's what he want to do."

They seemed to have forgot I was anywhere abouts. I don't know what got into me. "'Scuse me," I snapped. "Ain't nobody gotta go putting on no dress on my account. Y'all already done plenty to help this *white* boy." I jabbed my thumb at my chest. "Didn't ask nobody for no help, and I can doggone well take care of my own self. Been doing it for a long time."

Still holding the clothes, Miz Mancala shook her head. "As you wish. I thought the discord between the two of you was settled." She put the clothes in the trunk and went back to her rocking chair.

I glanced over at Calvin. He scrubbed the frayed edge of the rug with the toe of his shoe. *Me and my big mouth!* Mama had to be worried sick when she come home last night and I wasn't there, but I was still scared of Tugg and Jack. I wanted to take back my bluff. I shoved my hands into my pockets and stood there waiting for one of them to talk me out of it.

Finally, Calvin went to Miz Mancala and knelt down in front of her with his head down. "I's sorry, Miz Mancala. I didn't mean no disrespect."

A squeak come out when I tried to speak. I cleared my throat and tried again. "I 'pologize, too."

Neither of them paid me no mind. Miz Mancala cupped her hands around Calvin's face. "Do what your heart tells you is right, luv," she said. "Listen to the spirits, child. Allow them to speak to you."

"Spirits?" I looked around the cabin, hoping not to see no spirits floating about.

"Yessum," Calvin said, with his head still bowed and his eyes closed.

The old woman brought her hands to the top of Calvin's head. "Ori is master of all. It is Ori we praise. The rest of the body comes to naught. When Ori is missing, what remains is useless. What remains cannot carry our load. It is always Ori which bears the load." She took her hands from Calvin's head and held them out. Calvin put his hands in hers. Miz Mancala said, "Say the words with me. Ori I pray you."

Calvin repeated the words after her.

"Do not desert me; you are the lord of all things."

I finally figured it out. "Ori" had to be the name Miz Mancala called God. When Mama read to me from the Bible, that wasn't the name she called Him. I never heard no one call Him "Ori." I wished I'd paid more attention to what Mama read. Even though I wasn't much for praying, I bowed my head, too and asked God to help us. It was gonna take a real miracle to get us outta this one alive.

"Meditate on it, my child. You will know the right thing to do."

Calvin got to his feet, looking real down-in-the-mouth. "I do my best thinkin' when I'm fishin'. I'm gonna go catch us some catfish. This rainy weather we been having oughta have 'em hungry enough to jump on my hook."

I stood, too. "What if you run into Tugg and Jack?"

"I ain't forgot about them. I know how to stay outta their way, but we still gotta eat."

"Then I'm comin', too." I wasn't hankering to stay all alone with Miz Mancala, witch or no. "I ain't been fishin' since we left the farm." *Maybe I'd get a chance to sneak over to find Mama.*

Calvin wheeled. "Don't you never listen? I said I need to

think." He shoved his hands in his pockets. "Besides, I ain't got but one fishin' pole."

"I know how to make a pole from a willow sapling. An' you can think all you want. I'll keep real quiet." For a second, I forgot all about being mad at him. "I ain't really even got to have a pole. You got some string and a hook I can use? What kind of bait you got?"

Calvin looked at Miz Mancala. I reckon he was hoping she'd say I couldn't go, but she just shrugged like she read his mind. "You better keep quiet. I can't have you runnin' your mouth, scaring away all the fish. Or worse--getting us caught by them killers."

I pretended to lock my mouth and put the key in my pocket.

Huffing out a breath, Calvin shook his head. "Miz Mancala, it be all right if I take one of them biscuits?"

"Yes, of course, luv," she said.

With the biscuit in his shirt pocket, he headed for the door. I was so close on his heels, I nearly run into him when he stopped to get his cap and jacket off the nail on the wall. I took a step back as he turned around to speak to Miz Mancala. "Do there be anything you need us to do before we go?

"Not at all." She shooed us out the door. "Take care, mind you. Don't take any unnecessary chances."

"Yessum, I be careful," Calvin said. "I got a special fishin' hole nobody else know about but me."

I watched Calvin pull a cane pole and a rusty tin can out from under the porch. He laid the pole up on the floor and then dumped the can out beside it. It held a stick wrapped with string, some lead washers and several big fishhooks.

"What kinda catfish you aimin' to catch with hooks that big?" I asked.

Calvin glared at me over his shoulder. "I didn't see you pull no lip key outta your pocket."

I snorted. My breath made a little white cloud in the cold air. "Don't you ever give a straight answer?"

Finder's Magic

"Not if I can help it." He backed to the porch, put his palms on the edge and hopped up. His feet dangled over the side. I hopped up and sat beside him. Running his hand down the pole, he bent it back and forth a little, and then checked the string.

He handed me one of the hooks and the roll of string and jumped off the porch.

* * *

My pant's legs was wet to the knees from the melting frost by the time we got to the river. My feet and legs was freezing. Water squished in my shoes. The river flowed along, sluggish and gray. When we flushed a covey of Bob White quail and I thought my heart would stop. I jumped at every shadow and sound, all the while trying to keep a sharp eye out for Tugg and Jack and still keep up with Calvin, who seemed bound and determined to ditch me.

Calvin followed the bank, never uttering a word or looking at me. He stayed in the treeline and out of sight until we got to a creek that fed into the Peachtree. It was barely more than a trickle. He turned and followed it upstream through even heavier woods. About a hundred yards or more into the woods, it widened into a little blackwater pond. The swampy ground had a rotten, sour smell. The trees and brush around it grew so thick we couldn't see the river at all.

Calvin squinted up his eyes and said, "Don't you be tellin' nobody else about this place. You hear?"

"This is your great fishin' hole?" I looked around in disbelief. "Besides, who'd I tell?"

He gave me a disgusted look, sat on a rock and pulled the biscuit from his pocket. Twisting off a hunk, he squeezed it into a sticky ball. "You'll change your tune once them fish start hittin' your line." He mashed the wad of biscuit around his hook. "Now'd be a good time to use that key to lock up your lips again."

Finder's Magic

I shrugged and tied the hook he'd give me to the end of the string. "Could I have a couple of them washers to hold the line down?" He wasn't the only one who knew about catfishin'. Catfish is bottom feeders. I fastened the washers about a foot up from the hook. Calvin broke off another hunk of biscuit and handed it to me without me even having to ask for it. I rolled it around in my hand until it got sticky and pressed the hook into it. Once I unrolled the string, I wound up and cast the hook, bait and washers out into the pond. It sank fast. The water had to be way deeper than it looked. I tied the other end hard and fast to a low tree limb and sat on a log to wait. Calvin cast his line across the pond near some brush sticking up out of the water on the opposite bank. He jammed his pole in the ground between a couple of big rocks.

"That's a good way to lose a hook," I said.

Calvin glared at me.

I locked my lips. If he wanted to lose his hook, that was his problem.

He sat down at the base of a big tree and leaned back with one leg propped up on his other knee. He closed his eyes and pulled his cap down over them.

I sat on the log watching my line 'til my backside started to go numb. My pants was still wet and my feet and legs ached something awful. It was always cold working in the mill in winter time, but at least it was dry. I needed to move around and get warmed up some. I got up and checked the line where I'd tied it to the branch. While my hand rested on the line, I thought I felt the smallest of twitches. My eyes followed the line out to the water. Nothing. The surface was smooth as smoky glass. Must have been my imagination. Then he hit, nearly breaking the branch with the force.

"Calvin, I got one! A big one!" I grabbed the line.

My yell brought Calvin straight up. His cap flew off. He slipped on the wet moss and sat back down, hard. "Give him some slack." He scrambled to his feet. "And keep your voice down. We ain't that far from the river."

45

Finder's Magic

"I ain't got much slack to give him." The line had grown a mind of its own.

Calvin reached up and snapped off the branch I'd tied the line to. "Here," he said, handing the branch to me. "Work him 'til he gets tired."

I took hold of the branch with both hands, and took a few quick steps toward the water. That catfish jumped clean outta the water. *He was huge!* When he hit the end, I hauled back on it, setting the hook good and solid. Then that ol' fish dove to the bottom.

"Hoo-ee," Calvin said in a whisper. "Danged if you ain't got Daddy's ol' Jonah-fish."

I gave Calvin a quick sideways glance, but I was too busy trying keep the fish from breaking the line. I did wonder what in the world Calvin was yammering about, though.

Calvin rocked from one foot to the other, his fists clenched in front of him. I could tell he was itching to take over. "He's the one me and Daddy tried to catch when I was little."

I took a few steps back from the water's edge, being careful not to put too much strain on the line. The fish jumped again.

"He sho-nuf is a big 'un, now," Calvin said. "Daddy named him after that fish in the Bible. Said it was big enough to swallow me whole. Daddy tried everything to bring him in."

The way Calvin kept talking about his daddy, it dawned on me how much catching this fish meant to him. Well, I missed fishing with my papa, too. But I was the one what hooked this one--and I'd dang-well be the one to bring him in. That'd show Mister High-and-Mighty a thing or two. Even though I knew he was dying to grab the line, he stuffed his hands in his pockets instead.

The fish took off again. I planted my feet, braced for the coming jolt when he hit the end of the line.

Calvin jerked his hands out of his pockets. "You got to leave him some slack, or he'll break the line," He waved his arms like he was working the fish. "A branch don't have no give like a fishin' pole."

Finder's Magic

"I know what I'm doin'!" I gritted my teeth. *If only Papa was here to see me land this whopper of a catfish.*

I'd a done it too, but my feet slipped on the wet moss.

Calvin reached around and grabbed hold of the line. We had us a three-way tug-of-war – me, Calvin and that ol' Jonah-fish. Then something snapped and we landed on the soggy, mossy ground. Lucky for me, Calvin broke my fall. He wasn't none too happy about that.

"I told you to leave him some slack." He shoved me off. "Now look what you done. You let him get away." Calvin paced in a circle. "He's got the hook caught in his mouth where he can't eat. Now he'll die. What a waste!"

"I'd a brought him in if you'd left me alone," I muttered, and started rolling up the line. The weight on it felt like the washers might still be there. When I got to the end, not only was the washers still on it, so was the hook, but bent almost straight. "Holy smokes, would you look at this?" I held it up for Calvin to see.

Calvin's eyes widened. "Ain't nobody ever gonna catch that Jonah-fish." He stared out across the pond. He had a big ol' grin on his face.

Finder's Magic

Chapter Six

We never got another chance at the Jonah-fish, though we did catch a couple other good sized ones. Calvin caught two and I caught one. Neither one of us said 'nother word to the other while we was fishing. It had to be well after noon when we headed back to Miz Mancala's cabin.

I looked across the river at the mill workers' cabins. *What did Mama do this morning without me?* My thoughts turned to Papa and Jeb. I wondered if they had catfish ponds in heaven. I hoped so. A clear blue pond with the sun shinin' down.

When we got to Miz Mancala's, I carried in wood and water while Calvin cleaned the fish. Catfish ain't scaly like other fish, so you got to skin 'em. I took the skins and guts out and buried them away from the house. By the time I got washed up, Calvin had the fish sizzling in a big iron skillet on the potbellied stove.

"Boy, that sure is smellin' good," I said.

Calvin looked up and grinned, his face smudged with flour and cornmeal. "Just wait 'til you taste it. You gonna think you done died and gone to heaven."

Heaven made me think of Jeb again. It must a showed on my face, 'cause Calvin looked sheepish and mumbled, "Sorry."

That surprised me. Calvin could be nice when he wanted to. He pointed to a bowl on the plank counter under the kitchen shelves and said, "Hand me that bowl. I mixed up some hush-puppies to go with the fish."

I wondered where Calvin learned to cook so good, but I figured his mama or daddy had taught him. He still hadn't said nothing about his mama, so I figured she must be dead, too.

After we ate, Miz Mancala sat in her rocking chair sipping tea. It was late-afternoon when she asked, "Calvin, have you made your decision?"

Calvin didn't look up, but he said, "I'll go, Miz Mancala. I'll even wear that ol' skirt if you say so."

The old woman took a little bag tied with a string from around her neck. She held it out to Calvin. "I want you to wear this."

Placing the string necklace around his neck, Calvin said, "Thank you, Miz Mancala." He went to the trunk where the clothes were and put them on over his own. Miz Mancala pinned up the waist of the skirt for him.

"Ouch! Be careful with those pins!"

"So sorry, luv." She finished the disguise with a scarf tied around his head like a turban, and she did it all without being able to see a thing.

Calvin rolled up his pant's legs, so they wouldn't show under the skirt. If I hadn't watched him change clothes right there, I'd never recognized him.

Waving her hand toward a pie safe against the wall, she said. "There is a basket of eggs in the larder. Leave a few for us and take the rest to Hank's mother." She tapped one long finger on her cheek. "Let's see, we must be cautious of what we tell her. Too much information could place her in danger, as well."

That thought hadn't occurred to me. "Lordy, Miz Mancala, you don't think they'd hurt my mama, do you?"

"From what you lads have told me, they are ruthless men. If they see your mother as a threat, they would not hesitate to silence her."

Finder's Magic

I got a cold chill, remembering how they had *silenced* my friend Jeb, and knowing that's what they'd do to me and Calvin if they got their hands on us.

Miz Mancala laid her hand on Calvin's shoulder. "Tell Missus McCord that young Hank is safe, but he has something important that he must do before he can come home. Assure her that he will return as soon as he can." Miz Mancala went to the door and opened it. "Hank, please tell Calvin how to find your cabin."

"Yes ma'am." I looked at Calvin. "You know the place they call 'Cabbage Town'?"

"I know it," Calvin said.

"Our cabin is in the first row of cabins, last one on the left. It's a little one, just one room."

Calvin nodded and went out the door. I followed him out and stopped him on the porch. "The fish was real good. Don't worry about me telling no one about your fishin' hole."

He didn't say nothing.

"Calvin?" I said.

He finally looked at me.

"Thanks a lot. I owe you for this."

He whirled and shoved me against the wall, catching me completely off guard. The muscles in his jaw twitched. "Listen, don't go getting' the wrong idea. I ain't doin' none of this for you. I'm doin' it for Miz Mancala, 'cause she thinks it's the *right* thing to do."

My face burned. I thought we'd settled some of our differences and didn't have no idea what set him off like that. "What're you getting' so testy for?" I pushed him outta my face. "I was only trying to say thank you. What's wrong with that?"

Calvin turned away without saying another word. He hitched up the skirt and hopped off the porch.

I watched him trot off down the winding footpath, out of sight. "You make a ugly girl, anyways," I said, even though I knew he couldn't hear me.

Chapter Seven

Even from outside on the porch, the soft drumbeats seemed to bounce around in my head. Miz Mancala sang the same sorrowful sounding song we'd heard the evening before. I opened the door real quiet like so's not to disturb her, but she'd stopped singing and the drum sat on the floor where it'd always been. The cat wound around her ankles, and then curled up at her feet. That got me wondering...had she been playing the drum, or did I just imagine it?

She turned those pale eyes to me, as if she could see right through me. It gave me the shivers. "Hank, come tell me about yourself. Tell me of your family. Tell me your dreams, what you want life to bring you."

I sat on the floor, fiddling with my frayed shoe strings. I wasn't sure I wanted to tell that spooky old woman all about me and my family. "There ain't much to tell," I said.

She folded her hands in her lap. "We have nothing but time. Begin with your family. The rest will follow."

The first thing that come to mind was Papa's death, and then my secret. I wasn't about to tell her any of that, so I said, "Like Calvin said, my papa died. He got the lung fever last year on account of working at the mill. We used to be sharecroppers

Finder's Magic

before our barn burned down."

I watched her face to see if her expression changed when I mentioned the fire. It didn't...that I could tell. "I was pretty little, but I did my share of chores. We worked a little share cropper's farm near Milledgeville." I grinned, remembering something Mama said. "Mama called it 'Muddville,' 'cause we always come in muddy. She says I favor Papa on account of how I got his coloring and I'm a beanpole like him."

Miz Mancala's full lips parted in a smile. "Do you have brothers and sisters?"

"No ma'am. I'm the only one. Mama had two other babies, before me, but they died when they was first born. Mama said she knew right off I was gonna make it."

"How did she know this?" Miz Mancala asked.

My face felt hot. I was glad the old woman couldn't see me. "Mama says I'm special, 'cause I was borned on the first day of a new century. But I sure don't feel special."

"Is it because you no longer have your father?" she asked.

My throat ached. I nodded, but then I remembered she couldn't see me. "Yes ma'am. Me an' Mama work real hard at the mill. We do the best we can. We scrape by. I wish we'd just stayed on the farm. Maybe Papa would still be alive."

"Perhaps... What kind of work do you do at the mill?"

I was glad to talk about something else. "I'm a spooler. It's my job to make sure the weavers have full spools. If they run out of yarn, they'd have to shut down a whole line."

She smiled. "I can tell you are quite proud of the job you do."

"Naw, it ain't nothin' to brag about. They's lots of spoolers."

"And what of your dreams? Do you always wish to be a spooler?"

I thought of what Mama says about dreams. "Mama says dreams ain't for people like us. She said me and Papa was both dreamers. She says dreams is for rich folks, or folks with schoolin'. We ain't neither."

Miz Mancala shook her head. "What do *you* say, Hank

McCord?"

I don't know what come over me, I just started talking and it all come out. "I've always wanted to raise horses, ma'am. Me and Papa had this plan to raise them English Thoroughbred horses."

"Of course," Miz Mancala said. "Racing horses, the sport of kings."

"Well maybe we wasn't kings, but my papa knew horses. We even bought a mare, but we had to sell her filly. We named her Blaze 'cause she was a purty little sorrel--that's red--with a white streak down the front of her face. I been hopin' to save up enough money to buy her back." I remembered the feel of the wind blowing through my hair and the look of pride on Papa's face. I could barely swallow for the lump in my throat. "I still think about it a lot."

I didn't tell her my awful secret of how come we had to sell Blaze, or how Papa nearly died. *If I could buy Blaze back, maybe it would make up for some of it.*

Miz Mancala leaned forward. "Hold onto your dreams, Hank. Never lose sight of them."

"I've gone and messed everything up, now," I choked. "I'll be lucky to live to be growed, let alone go back to work, or save up enough money to buy a high-class horse."

She shook her head. "You are not to blame."

I was to blame, for part of it, but I couldn't bring myself to say so.

"It was meant to be, child. Everyone comes into this life with a special destiny. This is yours and you will be stronger for it."

Sure, if it don't kill me.

I didn't want to think about that no more, so I changed the subject. "What about you, ma'am? I can tell by the way you talk that you ain't from around here. Are you from England?"

Miz Mancala tilted her head to the side. "It was there I learned to speak the Queen's English. I was personal servant to my master's young daughter. When her tutor instructed, I listened as well. They paid me no mind."

Finder's Magic

"I knew it!" I said. "You sound just like some folks what visited the mill once. I heard they was from England."

She took a deep breath. "Yes, I spent a few years there, but my birth place was far away, in a hot, rainy little village in Cameroon in Africa on the Bight of Biafra. My grandfather was a very important man."

"Was he rich?" I asked, wondering how the granddaughter of such an important man would end up a slave.

The old woman threw her head back and laughed. "Money does not make one important, child. We were pitifully poor, by white standards. He was a holy man. People traveled many kilometers for his healing potions and his visions, even after his eyesight began to fail."

"You mean he was blind, too?" I never knew a single blind person before, let alone two in the same family... and with a blind cat, too. It set me to fretting. "Is it something catching?"

"Oh no," she said. "It is an affliction passed down in my family, though it occasionally skips a generation."

What a relief! At least I wouldn't catch something that might make me blind. Now if I could only keep from getting killed. Then I thought of something else. What did she mean by "holy man?" "You prayed for Calvin, but he said people say you're a, a..."

"Conjure woman? Witch?" She finished it for me. "People are afraid of what they don't understand."

"I believe in the Bible. My mama reads to me from it," I said, feeling full of myself.

Miz Mancala steepled her fingers under her chin. "That's good, but you should read *and* think for yourself.

"Yes ma'am," I said. I knew I should have left it at that, but Mama always said when I got something in my head, I was worser'n a dog with a bone. My curiosity overruled my manners and common sense. "I can't believe Calvin went out dressed like a girl. How'd you make him do that if you ain't no conjure woman?" As soon as I'd said it, I wished I hadn't. I didn't want to make her mad at me. *Who knew what kind of spell she might put on me?*

She didn't act mad. She just chuckled. "Calvin knows the right thing to do."

I'd gone this far, so I went on. "What was in that little bag you give him?"

"It is a talisman, or spirit bag," she answered. "It is to help protect him."

I didn't have no idea what a "talisman" was, but I thought to myself, if Calvin met up with Tugg and Jack, he was gonna need a lot more than some little bag on a string. He'd need some real flesh and blood muscles or some mighty fast legs. "I sure hope you're right, Miz Mancala."

Here he was putting his life on the line and he wouldn't even let me thank him proper. Well, I'd tried.

The cat raised his head and meowed softly. I heard the jingle of a wagon's traces outside, then the creak of the loose step. Even though I was expecting it, I jumped at the sound of loud rapping at the door.

Finder's Magic

Chapter Eight

Miz Mancala called out, "Who is it?"

"It jes' me, Willie Jordan. I brung yo firewood, like I promise. Cut an' split, ready to go straight in the stove."

"I'll be right along, Mister Jordan." She reached out and touched my shoulder. "Don't worry. You are safe. Mister Jordan can be trusted."

She opened the door to a wiry little old man, dark as licorice. He held his hat with gnarled fingers. The top of his head shone like a ripe eggplant, with a fringe of gray wool just above his ears.

Miz Mancala asked, "How is our Miss Bessie today?"

He rocked back and forth on bowed legs. "She much better, ma'am. The fever broke las' night, jes' like you say it would. She be eatin' eva-thing in the house today." He stood there grinning and shaking his head.

"That is indeed, wonderful," Miz Mancala said, clasping his arm. "You may stack the wood on the ground at the end of the porch." She turned to me. "Hank, kindly help Mister Jordan with the firewood."

I couldn't believe what she was asking me to do. It was taking a big chance letting someone else know where I was, but what else could I do?

When I walked out into the light, Mister Jordan's eyebrows shot up, but he didn't say nothing. He just nodded hello. I nodded back and kept my head down. After that he acted as if there wasn't nothing unusual about a skinny white kid coming out of Miz Mancala's cabin.

Mister Jordan sprang up onto his rickety wagon and began chunking wood to the ground. Hitched to the front of the wagon stood a big old bony gray mule. Both Mister Jordan and his mule looked ancient, but the old man moved like a youngster. When me and Mister Jordan finished stacking the wood, he took off his hat and walked back over to Miz Mancala standing in her doorway with her big yellow cat sitting at her feet.

"I sure does want to thank you, ma'am. I jes' don' know what I'd do if'n anything happen to my Bessie."

Miz Mancala's shoulders sagged. "I only wish there was more I could do for her."

Mister Jordan clutched his hat in his calloused hands, turning it 'round in a circle. "Yessum, I understands." He cleared his throat, then socked his hat on his head.

"And Mister Jordan," Miz Mancala said, "it is important that no one else knows of young Hank's presence here."

"Don't you worry 'bout a thing, Miz Mancala. You let me know when you runs low on wood, now. Me and Blue'll bring your some more." He went to his wagon and climbed aboard. It took him a few minutes to get his mule turned around and moving in the right direction. Mister Jordon looked back and gave us a wave.

I waved back, knowing Miz Mancala couldn't see him. I glanced over at her and was surprised to see her waving in Mister Jordan's direction.

"Miz Mancala?" I asked. "Did you pray a healing for Miss Bessie?"

"Yes, and I gave her some herbs to break the fever." She laid her long, thin hand over her chest. "There isn't much else to do. She is near her journey's end. Poor Willie will be lost without her." At that, Miz Mancala turned and went inside, leaving me standing, looking down the trail after Mister Jordan.

I began to think of Miz Mancala different then--not just a scary old blind conjure woman, but someone who really cared about other folks.

She called from inside. "Be a luv and bring in some firewood. I'll fix us a bit to eat."

I peeked in. She stood at the counter holding a big, wicked-looking butcher knife, the kind Mama used to lop off the head of Sunday's fried chicken dinner on the farm. On second thought, she was still plenty scary. I made a beeline to get the firewood.

Stacking the wood in the box by the stove, I asked. "What do you s'pose is taking Calvin so long? It ain't that far to our cabin. Ain't you getting' worried about him too?"

She just kept puttering around in her kitchen. "Have patience, dear. He will return."

"Yes ma'am, but what if he run into Tugg and Jack? And they recognize him? They're killers. Me and Calvin seen 'em." I imagined them beating Calvin so he'd tell where I was. They could'a been on their way to Miz Mancala's cabin right that minute. Why, Calvin could even already be laid out on the tracks, waiting for the next bone-crushing train. I shivered. Mama says when you get a shiver for no reason, someone just walked over your grave.

It was almost evening by the time we finished supper and I'd helped clean up. Calvin still hadn't shown up. I fretted and walked the floor.

The old woman didn't seem the least bit worried. She took down a board from a shelf. The board had two rows of scooped out places on it, six on each side and a wider one at each end. She also brought down a jar of smooth, shiny stones. "Let me teach you a game I learned as a young girl in Cameroon. Perhaps it will help to pass the time."

I weren't in the mood to play no games, but I did need something to pass the time. "What's it called?"

"Mancala," she answered.

58

"No ma'am, I meant the game," I said, thinking she misunderstood me. "What's the name of the game?" I spoke slow and loud.

Miz Mancala divided the stones into the little hollowed out places on the board. "I heard you perfectly well, dear. The name of the game is 'mancala.' As a youngster I was quite good at the game. So much so, my playmates substituted it for my proper name. I believe you call it a 'nickname.' I prefered Mancala to my slave-name."

That set me to wondering about her name, her *given* name. It'd never come to my mind how slaves had everything taken from them, even their own names. There weren't nothin' right about it. "Ma'am, if you don't mind me askin', what was your 'proper' name?"

She cocked her head. "No one has asked me in such a long time, I'd nearly forgotten. I was Saara. It means 'princess'."

I stared at Miz Mancala's creased old face and tried to imagine her as a young African princess. I'll just bet she was something. No wonder she carried herself like a queen. "That's a right pretty name. Why didn't you go back to it?"

She shook her head. "That was long ago. This is now." She ran her hand over the board and the stones. "This game is a lesson in life. You move the stones like so." She moved her hand in a circle over the stones. "The circle represents life. Each time you make the circle of life, you learn something, until you've reached your highest plane."

"What's that mean, 'highest plane?'" She was always talking in puzzles.

Miz Mancala picked up one of the stones. "This is you." She picked up another one from the same place and held them both on one palm. "This one represents Calvin. You are together on this plane for a reason. There is something that one of you must do for the other, something from your past that needs to be resolved."

"How can that be? We'd never laid eyes on each other before. The only problem I see is that Calvin don't like white folks much."

Miz Mancala sighed and put the stones back where she'd picked them up. "What is beneath the skin is the same for everyone. Before your birth, the gods planned the obstacles in your life."

What she was saying went against every thing I'd ever believed. There wasn't no way God would have planned the mess I was in. Besides, I always thought the devil was the one who give you problems. Mama did say that troubles make you stronger, though. I thought about how Calvin acted mad at me all of a sudden. "Miz Mancala, I ain't never done nothin' to Calvin. He offered to help me, and then he turned around and acted all mad at me."

Miz Mancala nodded. "I can understand how that would puzzle you. It is not you he is angry with, lad." She smiled a little, but her face looked sad. "Calvin has suffered much at the hands of white men."

"Well it ain't my fault," I sassed. "I didn't have nothing to do with whatever happened to Calvin." My friend Jeb suffered and died. Calvin was still alive, so I didn't figure he'd suffered all that much.

Miz Mancala changed the subject. "Let's play the game. Shall we? You may begin by choosing a group of stones on your side, and drop one in each space around the board." she explained.

My mama would'a had a hissy-fit if she thought I was doing some kind of gambling. It wasn't' really gambling, though. It was just a game. Least ways, that's what I told myself.

We moved each group of shiny pebbles across our side of the board clockwise, then to the other side according to the number of stones we picked up. The object was to get them all the way around to our own big cup, the one Miz Mancala called my "higher plane." The winner was the one who ended up with the most stones. Miz Mancala might have been old and blind, but that didn't keep her from beating the socks off me. She won almost every game.

"You must concentrate," she said after another win.

"Yes ma'am, but it's hard with it so dark in here. I can't even see how many little rocks are in my cups." Now that was a fool thing to say. I was getting beat by a blind lady. "Uh, I'm sorry Miz Mancala. You're right, I ain't concentrating," I confessed. "It's just that I'm real worried about Calvin." I got up and looked out the window once more. Still no sign of Calvin. My thoughts turned to Mama. What was she doing now? Had Calvin told her yet? *Where is he?*

She chuckled. "I suppose we could give you some light." Rummaging around her little kitchen, she said, "Now where did I put it? Ah, here it is." She picked up a lamp.

I was powerful glad she was gonna light a lamp. The darkness made me real uneasy.

"It feels as though there is sufficient fuel." She shook the lamp, sloshing the kerosene. "Would you be so kind as to light it, Hank?"

I rushed to get a piece of kindling from the stove. "I'd be glad to do it, ma'am."

As I lit the lamp, Miz Mancala said, "You have far more vision than you realize. It comes from within. Use your mind's eye."

There was them words again. I didn't have no idea what she meant by "mind's eye."

"You have the power of the world." Miz Mancala held her arms out wide. "Channel the strength. She brought her arms in to her chest like she was scooping up something. "Gather it and use it for good."

That just struck me as plum silly. "'Scuse me for saying so, Miz Mancala, but you don't know what it was like for me to see my best friend murdered and not be able to do nothing but run to save my own hide."

She took a deep breath and huffed it out. "I have not always been without sight, Hank. In my lifetime I've seen many injustices, and felt as helpless as you two children. For many years I was a bitter, angry young woman. It was not until I met an old slave woman who helped me return to my true faith that

Finder's Magic

I found peace."

I tried to picture Miz Mancala as a young slave girl. "How did you end up being a slave, anyway? I mean, with your grandpa such an important man and all."

"I was but a girl of ten years when I was taken from my family." Miz Mancala's voice quivered.

"Did you ever see your Mama and Papa again?"

She shook her head.

I had a sinking feeling that I might never see my own Mama again, neither.

Chapter Nine

Miz Mancala gathered the stones from the board and dropped them in the jar. She put everything on the shelf and come back and sat down in her rocking chair. She sat there so long without saying nothing, I thought she'd forgot all about me being there.

Finally she spoke. "On the day I was taken, I was playing with the other children in the compound of our little village." Sitting there, staring out with those blind eyes, she must have been seeing it all over again. Maybe that's what she'd meant by a "mind's eye." "A white man drove up in a cart. He wore a long, heavy black robe, even though our weather was always hot. He frightened me to the very bone."

I imagined him looking like Tugg Arnold. "What'd he do?"

"He spoke in broken Bantu, that was our language, inquiring of the whereabouts of our parents. Being the eldest, I stepped forward to speak with him. He put his face close to mine and spoke slowly and very loudly, as if I were hard of hearing, or slow-witted. Then he surprised me by asking if I was the daughter of Mulonda Mbuji, using my father's name."

The old woman crossed her arms over her chest, like she'd gotten cold. "He said I was to go with him. When I hesitated,

Finder's Magic

he grabbed me and carried me to his cart. Oh, I kicked and screamed like a banshee. He shook me viciously and slapped my face. He told me to be still. I looked about for the other children, but they had disappeared. Certain they had gone for help, I stopped struggling and waited to be rescued." She didn't say nothing for a few minutes. "Rescue never came."

"Was he a slaver?" I asked.

Miz Mancala cocked her head to the side. "Oh, no. He was a priest. He took me to the French mission."

"A priest kidnapped you?" I couldn't believe it. "Ain't they supposed to help folks?"

She chuckled, but her face didn't look happy. "He thought he was saving my heathen soul. There were children from other villages at the mission. I later learned that my father had given permission for me to be taken and educated in the mission. I hated him for that."

"You mean he gave you to the priest?" *How could a father give away his own daughter?*

Miz Mancala nodded. "The nuns scrubbed our bodies with harsh soap until our skin was raw. They put layers of stiff clothing on us to cover our bodies. I despised the feel of those binding garments. We had to rise before daylight to work in the fields, or in the kitchen. In the afternoons, we had lessons. I learned to speak French and German. In the evenings, we were forced to worship a god I knew nothing of. At first, I clung to the gods of my grandfather, but eventually, they began to slip from my memory."

"And English? You learned English there?"

"No, I would learn English later. This was a French Mission."

"But how did you end up being a slave?" I asked.

"I ran away from the mission. I was too angry and distrustful of my father to go home, but then I became lost. I was near death from thirst and hunger, when one night at dusk, I detected the aroma of food cooking over an open fire. Overjoyed, but near collapse, I staggered into the camp of men and women, whose

64

skin was dark, like mine. Hunger had so dulled my sense of caution that I failed to notice that most wore leg irons. The ones without chains carried guns."

"You mean colored people, like you, captured their own kind for slaves?" I couldn't imagine it.

"Sad, isn't it? They fed me, and then chained me with the others. I was too weak to resist. The next morning, the ones with guns herded us to the coast and packed us into the bowels of a slave ship bound for the Caribbean Islands. From there, the slavers transported some of us to Great Britain. I was one of the lucky ones. The ones who stayed in the islands had it much worse, I've been told."

It was dark outside, maybe as dark as the belly of that slave ship that took Miz Mancala way from her home. The fire in the stove was dying, so I got up and put more wood in it. An owl hooted from somewhere nearby.

"If they took you to Great Britain, how'd you end up in Georgia?" I asked.

Her rocking chair creaked. "The man who purchased me was a London merchant. Ironically, there was increasing opposition to slavery in Great Britain. It had become illegal years before, but many of the wealthy still held slaves. The master spent a great deal of time in 'the colonies' as he called this country. He eventually bought an American home. It was still legal to hold slaves in the United States. Here, I met a woman, another slave, who taught me what I'd only begun to learn as an African child, the faith of my fathers. She said I had the gift of healing, even then." Miz Mancala smiled her spooky sad smile and said, "Little did any of us know that war would come and free us." She sat there rocking and staring, unseeing at the wall.

I got up and checked the stove again, then walked over to the window. When Calvin's face suddenly popped up on the other side, I nearly passed out. "Lordy, Calvin!"

Calvin opened the window and climbed in. He had Miz Mancala's clothes rolled up in a bundle under his arm. He was shaking worse'n pine boughs in a windstorm. He scooted up close to the potbellied stove and held out his hands to warm them.

"Why didn't you come around to the door?"

His teeth chattered so hard I could barely understand him. "I d-didn't kn-know if'n the wh-white men g-got here ahead of me or n-not." He turned his back to the stove. "I w-was afraid they be watchin' the cabin. Real bad trouble's comin'."

"What's wrong?" I asked. "Did you see Tugg and Jack?"

"Yup, but they didn't see me, else I wouldn't be here to tell it. They got there ahead of me. They stirred everybody up. They made up a story 'bout how you and me beat up your friend and left him on the tracks to die... and how they tried to catch up with us, but wasn't able." He locked eyes with me. "Tugg showed 'em your cap. Said he found it near the body and that it was sure proof."

"Lord have mercy!" I didn't think things could get any worse, but they just had. We was being blamed for a murder we didn't have nothing to do with. But I needed to know, "Did you see my mama?"

"Yeah, but we don't have time for all that now. They's men coming with ropes and wearin' white hoods."

"Ropes?" I asked. My mouth went dry and my stomach cramped up worse'n when Mama makes me take a spring tonic.

Calvin's eyes looked hollow. "They always carrying hangin' ropes," he said.

Miz Mancala hadn't said a word since Calvin got there. All of a sudden, she stood up, threw a shawl around her shoulders, picked up her walking stick and went to the door. "There will be no hanging this night." She pulled the door open.

"Miz Mancala," Calvin called out. "Where you goin'?"

She didn't answer. She walked straight out into the dark.

Me and Calvin stood there looking at each other. "What got into her?" I asked.

"Miz Mancala know things," he said. "Maybe she seen a vision and know where them white men gonna strike."

"Well, she ought not to go wanderin' around in the dark," I said. "An old lady like her could get hurt."

"Calvin shook his head. "She's safer in the dark than you an' me. It always be dark for her."

"Well, I'm goin' after her." I grabbed my jacket and took out after Miz Mancala. I hadn't got more'n a half a dozen steps from the porch when I hooked my toe under a tree root and did a belly-buster on the ground. The air whooshed out all the way from my toes. Pain cut through to my back. I sat up and gulped like a landed fish.

Calvin got to me in an instant. He hunkered down beside me. "You all right?"

I croaked like a frog when I tried to answer him. "My back."

"Take it easy," he said. "You just got the wind knocked outta ya." I could see a flicker of light reflecting in his eyes even though there wasn't hardly no moon, only a sliver. Mama called that kind, a sickle moon. She always said, "No good comes on the night of a sickle moon."

No sooner had I remembered Mama's words, than I heard a commotion in the little shanty town, men's angry voices shouting, women and little kids crying.

Calvin groaned. "Oh no, they's already here." He jumped to his feet and charged into the dark woods.

I stumbled after him, trying to follow the sounds of his footsteps as best I could. The men's voices got louder. I couldn't hear Calvin's movements no more. Firelight flashed through the trees. The smell of kerosene was strong in the still air.

"Calvin, where are you?" I called in a loud whisper.

"Shh! I'm over here." He crouched beneath a big magnolia tree, its leaves black as coal, even in the flickering firelight.

I crawled up beside him.

Fire flashed, and a cross, at least ten foot tall, blazed up in front of the shanties. It lit up the whole place. Half a dozen colored men stood huddled together in front of their cabins. Women and kids peeked, wide-eyed, through windows glazed yellow from the burning cross.

Finder's Magic

As long as I live, I'll never forget that night. Miz Mancala stood like a statue between the cross and several men on horseback.

The men looked like spooky ghosts carrying flaming torches. They wore white hoods with eye-holes that looked black and empty. Even their horses wore hoods with big holes cut out for their eyes and muzzles. They could a come from hell itself, snorting smoke from their nostrils in the cold night air.

One of the horsemen spurred his horse straight at Miz Mancala. She calmly lifted her hand. Her mouth moved, but I couldn't hear any sound. The horse reared, dumping his ghostly rider. When his hood flew off, there wasn't no mistaking Tugg Arnold and his wavy, blond hair. He jumped up cussing and swinging his riding crop at his horse. I remembered the sting of that crop. The big horse jerked away, the muscles in his legs quivering. He was the same color as my filly, Blaze, golden in the firelight, deepening to blood-red in the shadows.

Some of the hooded men laughed. Miz Mancala's mouth moved again, but I still couldn't hear her. Tugg whirled and stomped over to her. He drew back his fist, like he was gonna slug her, but he looked scared. The men stopped laughing.

Calvin moved to stand, but I grabbed him and pushed him down. The colored men gathered around Miz Mancala.

I recognized Jack Little's high-pitched voice when he hollered, "Better leave her be, Tugg. She's that old blind witch."

Tugg cursed again and told Jack to shut up, but he backed away from Miz Mancala and the men who'd gathered around her. He picked up his hood and slapped it against his leg to knock the dirt off. One of the other men caught Tugg's horse and led it back to him. When Tugg stepped into the stirrup, the horse shied, nearly dumping him again. Tugg beat the horse's head with the handle of the crop and jerked the reins back. When he got the horse under control, he grabbed Jack's torch and stuck it close to Miz Mancala's face.

"Feel the heat, you old witch! You people can't hide murderers and get away with it. We'll burn down every shack, one at a time, 'til we find 'em." He tossed the torch through the open door of one of the cabins. Flames flared up inside.

Willie Jordan rushed into the blazing cabin, and got swallowed up by the smoke.

Finder's Magic

Chapter Ten

"That's just a sample of what's comin'," Tugg shouted. "You've got twenty-four hours to turn them criminals in, or we burn another shack." Tugg jerked the reins hard and spun the big horse around.

Tugg was acting all high and mighty, layin' Jeb's murder on me and Calvin, all the while he and Jack was the real murderers. And here he was burning homes of folks who didn't have nothing to do with him or the mill, and threatenin' worse. Any man who could do all that and mistreat a poor horse, to boot, was just sorry to the bone.

The white men rode out, whooping and waving their torches. Ribbons of flame and sparks from their torches faded into the black night.

Mister Jordan stumbled out through the flames and black smoke, a frail old woman draped in his arms like a worn-out quilt. Flames licked at the cold, black sky above the cabin. Sparks drifted over the trees, threatening to set the whole shanty town ablaze. Mister Jordan's neighbors lined up with buckets from the well to his cabin.

Calvin scrambled to his feet. "Come on!" he said. "It's on account of you an' me they done this. We got to help."

Finder's Magic

I stood looking down the road where the men in white hoods had gone.

"They ain't coming back t'night," Calvin said.

I prayed with all my might that he was right. Our lives depended on it. We stepped into the bucket line and helped pass the buckets of water. The heat from the flames was blistering. One of the windows blew out, showering us with slivers of red-hot glass. A woman screamed, reminding me of our mare's squeals the night our barn burned. The woman's skirt was on fire.

Calvin rushed to her and beat out the flames with his hands. I smelt burnt hair, just like that night in the barn. It made my chest ache, deep inside, clear to my core.

People eyed me with suspicious looks, but no one said nothing to me, or asked why I was there. We passed the heavy buckets until I thought my arms would fall off. The smoke filled the air so thick at times I couldn't see either end of the line. My eyes stung and my lungs felt like they would bust. My mind kept going back to that other fire.

Seemed like hours had come and gone, but finally a tall man closest to the cabin raised his hand. "Hold up on the buckets. Fire's out."

Everyone collapsed on the ground right where they'd stood in the line. I looked down at my arms and saw they was nearly as dark as Calvin's from the smoke and soot. A woman stepped out of one of the other cabins. We all looked up, waiting for her to speak.

She shook her head sadly and said, "She's gone."

A gasp went through the crowd. Miz Mancala's magic hadn't been strong enough to save Missus Jordan this time.

*   *   *

Friday, December 22, 1911

The next morning, the women folk took care of Missus

71

Finder's Magic

Jordan's body. Miz Mancala sent Calvin to fetch the bright colored skirt and blouse from her trunk because all of the dead lady's clothes had burned. The men built a coffin from pine planks.

The little church house looked like all the rest of the buildings with its gray weathered wood. The one thing that set it apart was the wooden cross on the roof and the graveyard next to it.

I felt about as welcome as the devil at a prayer meeting, so I stayed back out of the way. Standing outside, I listened to a man read some of the same Bible verses I'd heard my own mama read. When he stopped reading, a woman sang, her voice rich and mellow. The words of "Amazing Grace" rang through the open windows. After she sang, everyone joined in and sang "Swing Low Sweet Chariot," carrying Missus Jordan's coffin to the grave.

It all made me think of Jeb and Papa, 'til I couldn't hold back the tears. I'd never thought about colored folks much, but I could see they grieved just the same way we did.

Calvin come up beside me. "They say slaves used to sing that song." A muscle in his cheek twitched. "It meant getting set free." Clenching his fists, he said, "Death ain't no kind of freedom."

Finally, everyone left the cemetery except Mister Jordan. He stood there by the grave, tears streaming down his face. He didn't try to hide them, or even wipe them away. I took a step toward him, and Calvin said, "Where you think you're going?"

"I'm gonna go pay my respects to Mister Jordan," I said.

Calvin grabbed my arm. "You leave him be!"

"What are you so mad at me for?" I jerked my arm away. "It wasn't my fault. Besides, comin' here was your idea."

"Just leave him be," Calvin said again, and stomped away.

Calvin didn't have no business telling me who I should or shouldn't talk to. He didn't know nothing about me meeting Mister Jordan. It was only proper for me to go speak to him. It woulda been a whole lot easier to just leave, but my mama taught me better.

I spoke quiet as I could, but the little old man jumped when I called his name. He didn't seem to recognize me at first, then he gave me a weak smile and nodded. "I'm real sorry about your wife, Mister Jordan. I know you kept quiet about me on account of Miz Mancala, but I'm beholding to you, just the same."

Mister Jordan blew his nose and wiped his eyes. He took a shuddery breath. "Weren't none o' your fault. My Bessie weren't long for this world. She in a better place, now." He turned and looked at me with watery eyes. "Those be some real bad men. You watch yourself."

"Yessir, I will." I walked away, wondering where Calvin had stomped off to. He wasn't nowhere in sight, so I walked down to the riverbank and sat on a fallen log. I figured it was best to lay low and try to figure out what to do next. The river rolled along, same as always. It didn't care that my world was in a mess. I sat watching it for awhile. When I heard a rustling in the trees, I jumped to my feet ready to run. Calvin pushed through the brush. He stopped when he seen me.

I sat back down on the log. After a bit, Calvin sat down beside me. He picked up a little flat rock and skimmed it across the water. It bounced five or six times before it disappeared beneath the muddy ripples.

"I can't never get 'em to skip like that."

"It's all in the way you hold the rock." He picked up another rock, holding it between his thumb and first finger. "You gotta kinda curl your finger around it like this. The snap your wrist when you throw it." He let the rock fly. It skipped even farther than the first one.

I shrugged.

Calvin handed me a rock. "Here, you try."

Copying Calvin's movements, I snapped the rock over the water. To my surprise, it skipped three times.

"See," he said.

We sat there skipping rocks until Calvin said, "Remember I told you I know what it's like not to have nobody, or no place to go?"

Finder's Magic

"I remember. You told me your daddy was dead." I kept my face to the river, but watched him out of the corner of my eye, all the same.

Calvin stared at the river with his chin in his hand. "I don't remember my mama much. Daddy raised me best way he could."

"What happened to your daddy," I asked.

"They hung him."

"You seen it?" I gasped, sorry I'd asked.

He nodded and rubbed a finger at the corner of his eye.

"Who done it, Calvin?"

"Men in white hoods, like them last night. Maybe some of the same men." He took a deep breath. "Daddy heard 'em coming and woke me up. He set me out a back window." Calvin chewed on his bottom lip. "He told me to run and not look back."

"But why would they do such a thing? Did he kill somebody?"

Calvin glared at me. "He didn't do nothing. Some white girl come up missing. Her folks owned a feed store. They said my daddy had been hanging around. Shoot! All he did was go there to ask about a job." Calvin stared at the river. "They came in the middle of the night wearing white hoods. They drug him out and hung him in front of our house."

"Without even a trial?"

Calvin snorted. "Listen, you don't know nothing about how it is for us. My daddy never hurt nobody, let alone some ol' ugly white girl." He stood up and hurled a rock into the river. "She come home after they'd done lynched my daddy. She'd run off with a salesman. Guess he got tired of her and sent her packing."

I didn't know what to say. White men like Tugg and Jack had hung Calvin's daddy. Even though I didn't have nothing to do with what happened, I felt lower than grasshopper spit.

Calvin brushed his hands. "We got to go. Miz Mancala sent me to fetch you. She want to talk to us."

Chapter Eleven

Neither of us said a word while we walked to where Miz Mancala waited. I was still thinking on what Calvin had told me about his daddy. That had to be even worse than seeing your best friend killed and not being able to do nothing about it. I reckon that's why Calvin helped me. After watching his own daddy get killed, he had to know how bad I felt. And all that yelling at me about being a coward... Well, maybe he blamed hisself for not doing nothing to save his daddy. But, he was just a little kid. There wasn't nothing he could'a done. By then we was back at the cabin.

Miz Mancala sat in a chair on the rickety porch of one of the shanties, her shawl wrapped around her shoulders. Her face looked as calm as a willow pond in the middle of a hot summer day. But looks can sure be deceiving.

As we got close, Calvin called out, "Miz Mancala."

She motioned for us to come up onto the porch. "Sit with me," she said.

I had a bad feeling. We sat down at her feet and waited for her to speak.

"You understand you cannot stay here, now," she said.

Her words was like a punch to my gut. I looked at Calvin. He

Finder's Magic

had his head down, so I couldn't see his face.

Miz Mancala said, "Those men will not give up. They will be back."

My mouth went so dry I couldn't even make enough spit to swallow.

She swept her hand in front of her. "The people are frightened--with good reason. Someone is bound to tell where you are. It is up to the two of you to see justice is done."

If the grown-ups was scared, how did Miz Mancala think me and Calvin felt?

Calvin raised his head. His face was wet. "Miz Mancala, they'll kill us, just like they killed my daddy."

The old woman shook her head. "No, you must be clever. The spirits will protect you."

Calvin looked away, and then stood up. I turned to see what he was looking at. A tall woman walked toward us carrying a plate heaped high with food. Steam rose from it in the cold air. She gave it to Miz Mancala. She put her arm around Calvin's shoulder. "Come over to my house, sugar. The grown-folk got the house full, but you can set out on the porch. They's plenty more food. You boys worked hard as any of the men last night."

Calvin wiped his face on his sleeve. He looked at Miz Mancala. "I don't know."

Miz Mancala said, "Go eat. While there's still time."

That sure didn't make me feel a whole lot better.

Calvin turned back to the other woman. "Thank you Miz Lizbeth."

She smiled and gave Calvin's head a scrub with her knuckles. "I swear, you lookin' more like your daddy ever'day." She looked over her shoulder at me and said, "Come on, chile. Lord knows I ain't one to let no young un go hungry."

"Thank you ma'am." I said. I didn't feel much like eating right then, but I followed anyway.

We waited on the porch while Miz Lizbeth carried out plates of scrambled eggs, buttery grits, and big ol' flaky biscuits with more butter and dark, sweet molasses. She even brought us cups of strong coffee with lots of cream and sugar. "Way y'all worked, I reckon you's grown enough to drink coffee." She hurried back inside.

"Would you take a look at them cat's-head biscuits? They look almost as good as my mama's," I said.

Calvin looked at me like I'd sprouted horns. "What you talking about? What's a cat's-head biscuit?"

I picked one up. "Just look at it. It's big as a cat's head."

Calvin rolled his eyes. "That's 'bout the most feeble-minded thing I ever heard."

I was wrong about not being able to eat. Once I got started, I ate every crumb, then sipped the hot coffee. Calvin had a smirk on his face. "What?" I asked.

"Calvin pointed to his chin. "You got butter and 'lasses on your chin from your 'cat's-head' biscuit."

I wiped my chin and took a deep breath. I needed to say something serious to him. "Calvin, I'm sorry about what happened to your daddy. What them men done was wrong. I can understand why you wouldn't like white folks after that." I stopped to lick my sticky fingers. "I'm mighty obliged to you for helping me and riskin' your neck to go see my mama. Otherwise, she'd be fretting something awful by now."

He looked sheepish. "But I didn't get a chance to tell her," he said. "Remember, I told you, them two white men got there before I could."

"Tarnation, Cavlin!" My head snapped up. "What did they do? They didn't hurt Mama, did they?"

"Naw, but she acted real tore up about you getting in trouble with somebody like me."

I slammed my cup down, sloshing hot coffee on my hand. "Ow!" I wiped my hand on my britches. "She ought'a know me better."

Calvin squinched up his face. "You mean you too good to run with a colored boy?"

"Blast it, Calvin! That ain't what I meant at all." I jumped

77

up. "You gotta get that stupid chip off your shoulder. I meant she oughta know I wouldn't have no part in killing nobody, 'specially my best friend."

"Oh," he said.

"How can my own mama think I'm a murderer?" I paced back and forth. "I can't stand it, Calvin. I gotta get to her somehow. I gotta tell her what really happened." I paced back and forth.

Calvin shook his head. "There ain't no way. It's just too risky."

"Look, I know the back lots of the mill, prob'ly better'n Tugg and Jack. I ought to. I prowled around there for nearly a year before Papa got too sick to work."

He took a deep breath. "You gonna get us killed yet. Lord only knows why, but I reckon I'll go with you."

"Thanks, Calvin." Him offering to go with me when he didn't have to meant a lot. It give me a peculiar feeling, like we was supposed to do this thing together... or like we'd done and said all this before. I couldn't explain it, not even to myself. Calvin stared at me, kinda funny. Did he feel the same way?

Across the clearing some men had built a fire in a barrel and stood warming themselves around it. They smoked cigarettes and milled about, talking low. Ever once in awhile, one looked our way. I tapped Calvin's should and nodded in their direction. "I think it's time we got outta here. I don't like the way they're looking at us."

"Me neither," Calvin said.

We picked up our plates and cups and took them to Miz Lizbeth. When Calvin thanked her for the food, she hugged him. "You boys gonna be all right?" she asked.

"Yessum," Calvin said. "We gonna be just fine."

She followed us out onto the porch. She wiped her face on her apron and waved good-bye.

Calvin turned to me. "We better stop at Miz Mancala's cabin and get my fishin' pole. Maybe we can catch us some more catfish for supper."

"How can you even think of food?" I asked. "I'm full as a tick on a ol' hound dog."

"Yeah, me too, but I 'member what it's like to be hungry, too," Calvin said. "Ain't no tellin' when, or where, we gonna get out next meal."

We cut through the woods to Miz Mancala's the way we'd come the night before. Calvin pulled his fishin' pole out from under the porch. Then he crawled under and drug out a folded up tarp. "This'll keep us dry if it starts in to rain," he said.

We was just fixin' to leave when Miz Mancala come walking up the dirt path, her walking stick tapping the ground in front of her.

"We got to tell her bye and ask her to pray over us," Calvin said.

Miz Mancala's prayers hadn't been strong enough to save Mister Jordan's wife, but I didn't mention that to Calvin. Most likely, we was on our own from here on out.

Chapter Twelve

Miz Mancala's hands felt warm on my head. I tried to watch her face for some notion of what kind of vision she was getting from laying her hand on me. The creases on her forehead got even deeper.

"Calvin." She motioned him to my side. She kept one hand on my head and put the other on Calvin. She shivered, hard, as if she'd got a bad chill all of a sudden.

"What is it, Miz Mancala?" Calvin asked.

She let out a slow breath. "Cold," she said.

Cold like somebody who'd died?

As soon as she said the word, I felt the chill, too.

She took her hands from our heads. "There is danger in a high place. Remember this. You are strongest when united. Your strength is here." She touched Calvin's chest. "And here." She lifted her hand to his head again. "But most of all, here." She reached out taking one of my hands and one of Calvin's and put them together. "The two of you will remain strong, together." She squeezed our hands. "Remember."

I looked at our hands locked together, one dark, one light. I wondered what Mama would think of all this. Ain't no way she'd side with Miz Mancala. Mama wasn't uppity, but she believed folks ought to stay with their own kind. It was just the way things was with her. This one time, I had to go against what my mama thought. Way down deep, I knew Miz Mancala was right. The only way we was gonna get through this thing alive, was together.

Me and Calvin stayed in the woods, close to the river and his fishing hole the rest of the day. We made a tent in a dry spot by bending down a pine sapling, spreading the tarp over it and weighting the ends down with rocks. Calvin was purely a wonder. He knew all about how to live in the woods and stay out of sight. We piled brush and limbs around our tent to hide it. We took turns dozing and keeping watch all afternoon. I was dog-tired after fighting the fire all night at Mister Jordan's.

Calvin caught a catfish just before sundown. Our big breakfast was long gone by then and my stomach was gnawing on my backbone.

"We ain't got nothin' to cook it in," I pointed out. "Hungry as I am, I still don't want to eat no raw fish."

"Me neither," said Calvin. "That's why I'm gonna cook it."

"How?" I asked.

"Watch." Raking the dry pine needles away, he laid a circle of rocks. Then he stripped some willow bark from a tree. He shredded it real fine, 'til it looked like a little pile of hair. Next he propped some sticks over that in the shape of a teepee. Finally, he pulled two black stones from his pocket and struck them together. Each time they hit, they made sparks. The sparks landed in the willow bark hair and glowed. Calvin leaned over and blew on it. Flames flashed up and licked at the sticks until he had a hot little fire going. "Got to keep it low, so no one sees it," he said.

"Well, it's real good we got a fire, but what are you gonna cook the fish in? You got a skillet in your pocket, too?" I asked.

Calvin shook his head. "Don't need one." He grinned as he put a flat rock right in the middle of the fire. He took his knife from his pocket and slipped the blade right along the backbone on each side, and then pulled the bones out, slick as could be.

Finder's Magic

The fish sizzled when he laid it on the rock. I never smelled nothing so good.

We used flat pieces of pine bark for plates. I popped a hot, flaky piece of catfish in my mouth. "Fried tators and some of your hush puppies would sure go good with this," I teased.

"Humph! You want taters and hush puppies, that's your job. I got the fish." He talked around a mouthful of hot catfish.

"Where'd you learn how to do all this?" I asked.

"My daddy taught me most of it. Some of it I just figured out on my own, tryin' to stay alive after he was killed. Folks that knew my daddy, like Miz Lizbeth, fed me ever now and then. But they all had families to take care of, too. Then Miz Mancala took me in. I been with her ever since."

"How old was you when they hung your daddy?"

Calvin shook his head. "I don't rightly remember, but I was purty little."

"How old are you now?" I asked.

Calvin looked down at his fish and mumbled something.

"What? I didn't catch that," I said.

He straightened up and looked me in the eye. "I don't know how old I am. Wasn't nobody around to tell me when it was my birthday." The chip was back on his shoulder.

"Sorry," I said, and I meant it. I'd never knowed anyone who didn't know how old he was. Mama always made a fuss over me on my birthday. Not that we had money for store-bought presents or nothing. She'd always wake me up with a song and a hug. I felt sad for what Calvin had missed, not having no mama and then losing his daddy, too. I said, "You look about the same age as me, and I'm almost twelve. I just wondered 'cause you sure know lots of things."

Calvin shrugged and poked at the fire with a stick. I looked across the river. Lamps lit up here and there in the mill workers' cabins. Womenfolk was cooking supper for their families. Smoke and good smells drifted through the cold night air. It gave me the worst homesick feeling in the pit of my stomach. I missed my mama so much. Was she still at the mill, or at home

82

by now? Me and Calvin would have to wait 'til late at night to slip across the river without getting caught.

The later it got, the colder the air got. The dampness seeped into my bones, even as we huddled around the tiny fire. My hands and feet was nearly numb. My nose had lost all feeling and it was running. I stood up and stomped to get the feeling back into my feet.

Calvin said, "We got to get warmed up." He banked the fire with dirt.

"How in Tarnation are we gonna get warm if you put out the fire?"

"Help me roll these rocks inside the tent," he said. "Don't touch 'em. Use your feet, and don't let 'em get on the tarp."

I thought he'd gone plumb loco, but I did what he said. When we got the rocks in the tent, he pulled the opening together and laid a cool rock on the tarp to keep it closed. We sat close together with our feet on the hot rocks. Pretty soon, I stopped shivering.

I got to thinking how Mama used to pile so many quilts on my bed, I could hardly move. Then I got homesick all over again. "Calvin, you ever done something you was ashamed of?"

"I reckon so. Guess 'bout everybody done something they ain't proud of."

"Naw, I mean something real bad." I took a deep breath. "Something so bad it caused somebody to get sick and die?"

Calvin didn't answer for a minute. I couldn't see his face, but he was prob'ly looking at me like I was crazy.

"I don't recall ever doin' nothing like that," he said.

"Well, I did." I was glad he couldn't see *me*, now. "My papa died on account of it." The lump in my throat made it hard to swallow. I'd never told nobody the whole story, not even Mama. It was building up in me like a festered boil.

"Papa hired out for over a year to get enough money to buy a mare and breed her to a real good stallion. Me an' him had it all planned out. We was gonna raise them English Thoroughbred race horses, and train 'em. Papa said I had a natural way with horses." The lump in my throat moved to my chest as I remembered the mare and her foal.

"Her foal was the prettiest little filly I ever laid my eyes on. It was funny how I'd named her Blaze, and then she just about died in a fire. The barn caught fire and we couldn't get the mare out. She died. Papa breathed in so much smoke that he almost didn't make it out. The doctor said his lungs got blistered on the inside from all the heat and smoke. He never really got over it." I had to stop for a second, because of the lump in my throat. I swallowed and went on. "Papa traded Blaze to the man we rented the farm from to help pay for the barn. Papa's lungs was too weak to work at the mill, but he done it anyway. Now he's gone, and I can't even go home without getting killed, myself."

"That don't make it your fault he died," Calvin said.

"You don't understand," I snapped. "I'm the one who started the fire." There, I'd said it... finally. I was real glad it was dark in that tent. "I was supposed to be doing my chores, but I'd stole some of Papa's tobacco and some matches from the kitchen. I had to hide to smoke it, 'cause I wasn't allowed. I hid in the back stall of the barn. I tossed the match down without thinking anything of it. I didn't know it was still hot enough to start a fire. It must'a smoldered in the straw for a while, because I didn't notice 'til it was burning big." I could almost feel the heat and smell the smoke. "If I'd watered the horses first, like I was supposed to, at least there would'a been water to throw on the fire. There wasn't even half a bucket of water. An' I spilled more of that than I got on the fire." I wiped my nose on my sleeve.

"The mare went wild. Papa heard her squeals and run out from the house. She almost sounded like a woman screaming. Papa tossed me a rope and told me to get Blaze out. I thought that mare was gonna kill me or Blaze before we could get outta that stall. The smoke was so thick I couldn't see anything by then. Somehow I managed to drag Blaze out of the barn."

My eyes burned and tears rolled down my cheeks. "Papa told me later the mare choked on the smoke and went down. He had to give up on her when the rafters started coming down.

He barely made it out by crawling on his hands and knees. But he'd breathed in so much smoke, he fell out on the ground outside. His face and arms was burned bad." I sucked in a ragged breath.

Calvin hadn't said nothing else all this time I was talking.

"He could have died in the fire, Calvin. I about killed my own papa." I buried my face in my hands and sobbed. "It wasn't working at the mill that killed him. It was me." It hurt something awful to remember, but somehow it felt better to get it off my chest. I could barely feel Calvin's hand patting my back.

Finder's Magic

Chapter Thirteen

When I woke up, I didn't have no idea how long I'd slept. At first, I didn't even know where I was. It was dark and cold and I didn't want to move, but the bed seemed as hard as the ground. My whole side ached. The cabin window wasn't where it was supposed to be. I rolled over to my back and bumped into Calvin. He mumbled in his sleep, and then I remembered everything that had happened. *If only it all coulda just been a bad dream and I'd woke up at home.*

"Calvin, wake up," I said, shaking his shoulder. "I think it's late enough now."

"There's too many. We'll never make it." He took a swing at me.

It's me, Calvin! It's Hank."

He jerked awake. "Huh? Aw, I was havin' a bad dream."

"Yeah, me too. But it's real."

"No! There was this big battle, with guns and cannons. I was pinned down in a ditch and couldn't move. Then you come charging in on a big red horse, leaping over the ditch." Calvin ranted on, breathing like he'd been running. "You had this long rifle, with some kind of spear on the end of it. When you shot, fire flashed out from the barrel. I scrambled out of the ditch and you reached down and swung me up behind you."

I got that funny feeling again, like I been here and heard the words before. I couldn't make no sense of it. I tried to calm Calvin down. "It was just a dream, Calvin. It sounds like one a them Civil War stories my papa used to read to me," I said.

"But it was so real," Calvin said.

"That's the way dreams is sometimes. Now let's go see my mama."

When we crawled outta the tent, I was jolted by how much colder it'd got. It was a lot worse than before. My teeth commenced to chattering like crazy. The sky was clouded over and not a star in sight. We walked fast and pretty soon I didn't feel as cold. The gaslights across the river lit up the undersides of the clouds with an eerie orange glow. "What's the matter?" I asked when Calvin stopped at the bridge.

"We better split up for a little bit. We gonna draw too much attention together," He said. "You go first. I'll start across when you get to the other end."

"All right," I agreed. "I'll wait over in the alley by the beer hall."

"Good idea," he said with a grin. "Them men coming outta there ain't gonna pay no mind to a couple of boys, no matter what color their skin is."

The beer hall was bustling. I remembered what day it was. It was Friday. *Payday!* The mill owed me money. I stood in the alley at the corner of the beer joint. A tall skinny fella come out, hanging all over a lady. The lady had on a dress that left a whole bunch of her uncovered. She had a lacy shawl over her shoulders. She had to be about to freeze. The lamplight shimmered off her golden-blond hair.

The man tried to steal a kiss. The lady didn't seem to mind. She just pushed him away, giggling and said, "Hold on, sugar. There'll be plenty of time for that when we get to my place."

"Just one little kiss to tide me over, darlin'. His words was slurred. My skin crawled at the sound of Jack Little's voice. He had something tucked under his arm. He shifted it and I could

Finder's Magic

see it was a little cream-colored puppy. It whined and wiggled and Jack almost dropped it. Jack lifted it up to his face. "It's all right, little feller. Ol' Jackson gonna take real good care of you."

The lady giggled again and reached out to pet the puppy's head.

Just then, Calvin come walking up the boardwalk. He stopped and stared at the lady. I didn't know what got into him. There was Jack Little no more that a few feet from him, but Calvin stood frozen in his tracks. Lucky for Calvin, Jack was in no condition to recognize anybody.

"Psst, Calvin!" I whispered as loud as I dared.

Calvin finally snapped out of it. He turned his head this way and that, looking for me. Jack and the lady staggered toward him. Calvin sidestepped into the ally, nearly bumping into me before he spied me.

"That was close," he gasped, wiping his forehead.

"What was the matter with you?" I scolded. "What if Jack recognized you? You know what he would do to you."

There I was lecturing Calvin about staying clear of Jack when I heard what Jack said to the lady.

"Don't you worry, darlin'. I got plenty of money tonight." He patted his jacket pocket.

That really set me off. Jack Little had extra money, and I didn't have none, even though I'd worked most of the week for it. It was payday and somebody owed me some money. I eased up on the sidewalk, staying close to the wall in the shadows and followed Jack and the lady. I was breathing hard, my breath making fog. I started to sweat, cold as it was. Somehow, I was gonna get what was owed me.

"Where are you going?" Calvin followed me, close on my heels.

"Shh," I hissed.

Jack and his fancy lady went to an old two-story house a little ways down the street. It had stairs on the outside. She had a devil of a time trying to help Jack up the stairs. About halfway up, Jack missed a step and somersaulted all the way down, almost taking the lady with him. She come running down after him hollering, "Oh lordy, lordy!"

She knelt beside him, laying her hand on his chest. "Oh sugar, are you all right?"

Jack sat up. He had a dopey grin on his face, but he still held the puppy cradled in his arms. He managed to hand to puppy to the lady. "Take care of our little one." He snickered and said, "Jack and Jill with up the hill to fesh..." His eyes rolled back and his head thumped on the ground.

Lord forgive me, but I wished him dead. Dead as my papa and Jeb.

The lady sat the puppy on the ground where it commenced to whining. She dug her hands into Jack's pockets and pulled out a wad of money. Without thinking what I as doing, I rushed over to the lady.

"Is my daddy dead?" I cried. I was so scared, I didn't even have to fake the tremor in my voice. My heart was pounding something awful.

The lady looked up at me, her painted lips in a red "O".

I wiped pretend tears. "Mama was afraid of something like this. That's why she sent me lookin' for him." I whimpered and wrung my hands. "We ain't got no food in the house and my baby sister's bad sick with the croup." I started in wailing louder.

The lady said, "Hush up, darlin'. Hush now. It's gonna be all right. Look, here. Take this to your mama. Y'all need it more'n I do. And look, your paw even got you a puppy."

She stuffed the roll of money in my hand. It was a whole lot of money. "Wait." She peeled off one of the bills, and stuck it down her dress, in between--well, in the front. "This'll take care of his board for the night." She gave me a hug and patted my cheek. "You go on home to your mama, now. And don't grow up like your paw." She smelled like flowers and cigar smoke.

"No ma'am, I won't." I sniffled and stuffed the roll of money in my pocket. I jumped up and hightailed it outta there before

89

Finder's Magic

Jack come to.

"Wait, you forgot your puppy," she called after me. "And don't worry about your paw. I'll get some of the men over at the beer joint to carry him to the back room. He can sleep it off there."

I turned around and waved. Under my breath, I answered, "Thanks, but you can drop my 'paw' down a well."

"'Scuse me, sugar? What did you say?"

I bit my lip to keep from busting out laughing. I said, "Thanks to you an' Paw, my sister's gonna get well." I raced around the corner where Calvin hid and motioned for him to follow.

We didn't slow down 'til we got out back of the livery stable. A lamp in the office upstairs gave off a soft light through the window. I had to see how much money the lady'd shoved into my hands. Calvin leaned over my shoulder, counting along with me as I peeled off the bills.

Calvin let out a soft whistle. "Ooowee! That's two hunnard and twenty dollars. Where did that fella get so much money?"

"He must'a been gambling and got lucky's all I can figure. No way Jack earned this much money working at the mill." I divided the money. "Half is yours." I held the money out to him.

Calvin shook his head. "Hunh uh! I get caught with that much money, I gonna be swingin' from a tree for sure. Nobody gonna believe I came by it honest...which this ain.t".

"So, we just don't get caught with it," I said. "Either we get someone to keep it for us or we hide it." I couldn't keep from grinning, even though it was wrong to take something that didn't belong to us. I rolled the money back in a tight wad and stuck it in my pocket. The weight of it felt real good.

Calvin shook his head and grinned, too. "You one crazy white boy."

A horse in a pen back of the stable nickered and pawed the ground. I looked around. He was snubbed up close to the fence and couldn't reach feed or water.

"Look at that," I said. "I like to do the same thing to the

sorry so and so who left him tied up that way." I snuck over the fence, slow and easy, so's not to spook him. When I got closer, I recognized the horse. It was Tugg's big sorrel.

I stepped up on the bottom rail. The horse's eyes looked wild, and he tried to pull back on the rope. "Easy, big guy. Easy," I crooned. "Nobody's gonna hurt you." The skin on his neck twitched when I stroked it. "See, that's not so bad." I could feel his muscles relax just the least little bit. He didn't move when I climbed through the rails. I kept talking to him as I untied the rope from the fence post. He followed me, gentle as a lamb to the water trough and stuck his nose in the water. He drank and drank. No telling how long he'd been tied like that. I couldn't believe the livery man would let anyone leave a horse like that. Anybody knows better.

The stallion finally raised his head. He shook and blew water from his nose, spraying me good. "Hey!" I laughed and wiped my face with my jacket sleeve. "That's no way to say thank you." I reached up to pat his head, but he dodged. I knew he'd had some mighty rough treatment at Tugg's hand. I lifted my hand slower, and he lowered his head to me. I combed my fingers through his tangled forelock and scratched his ears. His eyes drooped halfway closed. He pushed his head against my fingers, getting the most out of the rub.

Calvin stood there watching. "You gonna stay in there all night pettin' that old horse? We better get a move on, 'fore we get caught."

I could'a stayed there all night, easy. It almost felt like going home, breathing in the sweet smell of hay and horses. Calvin was right, though. It was too dangerous to stay there. I thought about turning the horse out, but Atlanta was a dangerous place for a runaway horse, so I left him loose in the pen. I tossed a block of hay over for him. He tore off a chunk with his powerful jaws and watched me climb out of the stall. He nickered as me and Calvin walked away. I wished we could take him with us, but I didn't need to add horse thieving to my list of crimes.

Finder's Magic

* * *

Saturday, A.M, .December 23, 1911

We was almost to the mill workers' cabins when I noticed a light come on in a window. People was already stirring, getting ready for work. I had fooled around too long. Mama always left way before sunup. Still, I had to find a way to get word to her.

"Uh oh, it's later than I thought," I said.

"Uh huh. If we hang around 'til the sun's up, I gonna stand out like a peppercorn in a salt shaker over here."

"You go on back to our camp. I'll meet you there. I got to get word to Mama, somehow."

Calvin shook his head. "Miz Mancala say we need to stick together."

"No, she said we was stronger when we worked together. That's different. We'll still be working together."

Calvin seemed to be having a hard time making up his mind. "What you figure on doin'?"

"I'm just gonna slip home and leave some of this money and a note for my mama."

"All right," Calvin said. "But don't be takin' no more crazy chances."

"Better be careful." I smirked. "People gonna get the idea you like me."

Calvin snorted. "Humph! I liked you better 'fore I knowed you was a lunatic." He walked away... toward the river.

Chapter Fourteen

It seemed like a dozen years had passed since I'd been in our little cabin. It's hard to explain, but I wasn't the same boy who'd left that cabin only a few days before--not after seeing Jeb murdered and having to run for my life.

The stove was still warm. I lifted the lid of Mama's big cast iron Dutch-oven on top of the stove. Inside, rolled up in a clean dish towel was two thick ham biscuits. We hardly ever got ham, but Mama made the best biscuits in the world. *She knew I'd come home.* My mama still loved me. The biscuits was proof. I took one out, wrapped the other one back up and stuck it in my jacket pocket for Calvin.

I looked for something to write on. There wasn't no paper or nothing. Then I thought about the piece of paper Tugg had dropped. I dug it out, then decided it was too little for all I needed to say, so I stuck it back in my pocket With a piece of charcoal from the stove, I wrote on Mama's clean plank table, while I devoured the biscuit. If she'd been there, she'd a give me a smack for making such a mess. But if she'd been there, I wouldn't had to leave a note on the table.

Finder's Magic

Dear Mama,
I am fine. Don't wory. I aint done
nuthin bad.   The mony is ours. By what
you need and somthin nice for yorself.
Yor son, Hank.
P.S. Thanks for the biskits.

If I'd left too much money, Mama woulda thought I'd done
something bad, for sure, so I only left ten dollars. It would
be enough to buy some groceries and maybe a pretty piece of
calico.

Papa's coat and hat still hung on a peg by the door, like he
was coming back any day. I slipped his coat on. It was a lot
warmer than mine and maybe nobody'd know me in it. The
sleeves was too long, so I rolled them up. When I turned the
collar up, I could still smell his pipe tobacco. I put his hat on
too, pulling it down low over my eyes. It was time to get moving
before I started bawling. Making sure no one was around, I
snuck out and headed for the river, lickity split.

The bridge was the most dangerous part because there
wasn't no place to hide. I was about halfway across when
a wagon pulled up beside me and slowed down to a crawl. I
tugged Papa's hat down some more and dropped my chin into
the collar of his coat.

"Whoa, Blue." Mister Jordan pulled his bony mule up. "Lawd
have mercy, boy! What is you doin' out here?" He looked over
his shoulder. "Git in the back and cover up with that tarp."

I looked up so fast, Papa's hat nearly flew off. Doggone if
Mister Jordan hadn't seen right through my disguise. Him and
Blue was a mighty welcome sight, but I didn't want him to get
in more trouble. "But Mister Jordan, if Tugg and Jack catch
you with me in your wagon..."

"Hush up! Don't argue, an' don't be dilly-dallying."

I scrambled into the back of his wagon and crawled under
the tarp.

"Gid-up, Blue."

Blue leaned into the harness and the wagon rocked forward. "Atta boy, Blue. They's a bucket of sweet corn a waitin' for ya at the end of the trail." Mister Jordan commenced to singing. It wasn't no song I knew. It sounded like he was making it up as he went.

All time haulin' de wood, me and big Blue.
Hauls it up an' down, all the whole day through.
What ya gonna do with a mule like Blue?
Don't-cha know, Blue he got a trick or two.
Winkin' his eye when the freight train come through,
He say, dat's where dey gone, dat boy an' you.
Now dey done gone south where da sky am blue.
Oh yeah, way down south, where da sky am blue.
Oh yeah, oh yeah. Dat's where dey done gone to.

"Whoa now, Blue." Mister Jordan pulled the big mule to a stop. "We's far enough away from the mill now, boy. Where in the ever-loving world was you agoin'?" Blue shook, rattling the traces and pawing the ground.

I lifted the tarp and peeked out. "Thanks for the ride, Mister Jordan. Me and Calvin got us a camp hidden back in the woods. I reckon it's safer for you if you don't know just where." I slipped over the side of the wagon to the ground. "Was you just making up a song, or did you really trick Tugg and Jack into thinking me and Calvin hopped a freight train?"

Mister Jordan snickered and shook his head. "Dey jump on it like a fish on a worm. Blue had a mighty hard time keepin' a straight face, don't ya know. The two a them prob'ly half way to Macon by now, lookin' for dat boxcar y'all s'posed to be in." He pushed his hat back with his thumb. "Don't you worry 'bout me an Blue. We been around long enough we done 'bout seen ever'thing. You needs something, you can count on us." Blue

Finder's Magic

pawed the ground again.

"Awright Blue. You know the corn be awaiting for ya." Mister Jordan clucked and slapped the reins lightly on the mule's bony rump. He drove off singing his made-up song.

I cut back through the woods to the edge of the river and our camp. We'd done such a good job hiding it, I almost walked right past the tent. Nothing looked like it had been messed with. I snuck over and lifted the back side of the tarp. Calvin wasn't there.

I stood up and turned around. There stood Calvin, smack in my face. "Aaak! Don't do that!"

"Do what?" Calvin had that irksome grin on his face.

"You know what! Don't sneak up on a fella like that." I took the biscuit out of my pocket and waved it under his nose. "I got a good mind not to give you this ham biscuit my mama left for us."

His eyes locked on the biscuit. "Your mama made biscuits for us? With ham?"

I pulled the dish towel back. "I already ate one, but I could sure go for another one."

His hand snapped out, quick as a rattlesnake and snatched the biscuit. When he bit into it, he closed his eyes. "Ummm. What'd she say about Tugg and Jack?" he asked with his mouth full.

I shook my head. "She was already gone to work. I didn't get to talk to her, but I left her a note.

"How'd she know you'd come?" he asked.

I shrugged. "Maybe she just hoped I'd come. Listen," I said. "I saw Mister Jordan. He told Tugg we hopped a freight train to Macon. He thinks they believed him and went lookin' down there for us."

"Naw, that fella, Jack is still here. We seen him last night."

I nodded. "Tugg musta left Jack behind to keep an eye out for us, just in case we didn't hop a train."

Calvin swallowed. "That old man got a lot of spunk. Least ways, they won't be burning no more cabins tonight."

"Yeah," I said. "And that gives us a little time."

"Time for what?" he asked, squinting his eyes and chomping into the biscuit again.

"I been thinking about the things Tugg said to Jeb."

"Like what?" Calvin asked.

"I ain't figured it all out yet, but Tugg kept asking him who else he told about their *operation*. That could only mean one thing--they're up to something outside the law."

"What's that got to do with us?"

"If we can figure out what they're operation is, we can take proof to the sheriff."

Calvin stopped chewing, a wad of biscuit still in his cheek. "You know how I feel about going to that white lawman."

"No, listen," I said talking fast. "If we had proof, we could take it to Mister Murphy, the mill owner. Then he'd believe us when we tell him they killed Jeb. While Mister Jordan's got Tugg off chasin' after freight trains, we can go snoop around their office. I just know we'll find some lead to what Jeb knowed."

Calvin chewed fast and swallowed hard. "I was afraid you was gonna say something crazy like that."

Then I remembered the paper Tugg had dropped.

Finder's Magic

Chapter Fifteen

I dug it outta my pocket again. Weren't nothing else in there but strings and lint... and the money. We had to hide the money soon!

Me and Calvin read the names on the paper over and over again. They was all names of kids what worked at the mill. We couldn't puzzle it out. Still, I had a gut-feeling that it was important, somehow. Then I got a idea on how to get the drop on Tugg and Jack.

We hid the money I stole from Jack in the hollow of a dead oak tree. Calvin tried to talk me outta my plan, but he finally come around to my way of thinking, even though it could be mighty dangerous.

Calvin tried fishing, but he only caught a couple of little crappies. We cooked 'em on the rock, same as before, but they was bony and stringy, not near as good as the catfish. Laying low the rest of the day, we put our heads together to come up with a way to get to the mill without getting caught. Whatever we did, it'd be best to wait 'til after quitting time, when nobody was around. Finally, Calvin figured out a way we could do it, but we would need the help of Mister Jordan, his wagon and Blue.

"He might send us packin' though, for all the trouble we done caused him," Calvin said.

Late that afternoon, we snuck over to Mister Jordan's burned out cabin. He'd pitched a tent, too. His was a real one, though, not just a ragged tarp slung over saplings. Blue stood tied to a hitching post while Mister Jordan brushed him down. You'd think Blue was a fancy race horse, the way that old man took care of him.

Mister Jordan grinned like he was glad to see us. "Y'all come on in the tent, out of sight," he said. That sounded like a good idea.

When we laid out our plan, he agreed to help us. Calvin was right; Mister Jordan had a lotta spunk for a old man.

The three of us stacked a load of wood on his wagon. It wasn't a full load. Mister Jordan showed us how to place the wood so it looked like a full load, with a space for me and Calvin to hide underneath. That old man knew just how to do it. It got me wondering what else he might'a hid under the wood in his wagon.

He hitched up the big mule, talking to him all the while. "Don't you fret, ol' friend. Dis ain't no heavy load. We be back in no time a'tall. Dey gonna be a special treat when we gets back. You'll see."

Me an' Calvin crawled in the tight little hidey-hole under the wood. Mister Jordan closed the opening with more wood. I took a deep breath. It smelled of fresh-cut pine and moss. The wagon rattled and bounced over the wooden bridge. I feared we'd get squashed if the wood shifted. Luckily, it stayed put, and so did we. I heard the whistle at the mill. *Quitting time.*

Mister Jordan drove right up to Tugg and Jack's office across the tracks from the main millworks. The wagon rocked a little when Mister Jordan hopped down. We couldn't see much from under the wood. We heard him knock on the door. "Helloo, inside. I got's y'all's firewood here."

There wasn't no answer. I breathed a sigh of relief.

Next thing I knew, Mister Jordan pulled away a couple of

logs and peeked through the opening. "Awright," he said. "Nobody here."

I climbed out behind Calvin. My legs felt shaky. I went around to the side of the office and tried a window to see if they'd left it unlocked. No such luck. I was fixin' to go around to the other side, when Calvin's face popped up--inside.

"How'd you get in there so fast?" I asked.

Grinning from ear to ear, he tapped his noggin. "I done used my head, like Miz Mancala say." He held up a piece of wire. "I picked the lock. Now hurry up an' git in here."

Inside, we searched for some kind of clue to tell what Tugg and Jack was up to. I didn't have no idea what to look for. I gave Tugg's cluttered desk the once over. A long skinny book lay open on top of the piles of paper. I flipped through a few pages. It was hard to read his hen-scratchy writing. Down one side was a list of names. I knew a lot of the names. They was all mill workers, like me. The other side had a line of numbers. It all looked real businesslike, which confounded me. I hadn't figured on Tugg and Jack being that smart.

Calvin stirred in the wood box.

"What are you doin' over there?" I asked.

"I thought it might be a good hidin' place for valuables... or incriminatin' evidence," he said.

"Now where'd you learn such big words?" I waved him off. "'Bout the only thing what hides in wood boxes is rats. Now get away from there." I rummaged through more papers on the desk. "Come help me look for clues."

A soft whine come from a box in the corner and Jack's little cream-colored puppy poked his head over the edge. The box tipped over and he waddled out to greet us. He stopped and made a puddle in the floor. I couldn't help but laugh and he padded over, just a wiggling.

Calvin stopped stirring in the wood box and reached down. "Say now, looky here!"

"Don't you bring no dead rat over here!" I scolded. "I done told you before, I can't abide rats."

Finder's Magic

Calvin pulled a flat metal box out from under the wood. "What you reckon this be hid for?" he asked.

"Let me see that!" I grabbed the box from Calvin's hands.

The box wasn't locked. It just had a cotter pin through the hasp. Inside was another book, like the one on the desk. I picked it up. Under the book was money...a whole pile of money!"

"Jumpin' Je-hosophats, Hank!" Calvin gasped. "I never seen that much money in my whole life!"

I opened the book. It had the same hen-scratchy writing as the other one. Calvin leaned over my shoulder. "It just looks like a list of names," he said.

"Names!" I sucked in a breath. *Tugg's list of names and numbers.* I pulled the paper from my pocket and straightened it out. "Look at this." I shoved the paper under Calvin's nose. "It was written by the same person--and some of the names are the same ones in that other book."

Calvin pointed to a ragged edge in the book. "They's a page missing right here."

"You know what I think?" I asked.

Calvin shook his head.

"I think these are some kind of payroll books. And Jeb found 'em and tore out this page."

"But why would they have two, just alike?" Calvin asked.

"I don't know." I ran my finger down the list of names. "Hey, they ain't exactly alike." I pointed to my own name and the number to the side. "See, this date's the same, but the numbers are different."

I slapped the book closed. "I think Tugg and Jack been stealin' from the workers. Not everyone, mostly kids. Especially kids that don't have no other family workin' here. Or maybe the ones they think ain't too bright, like me. That must be what Jeb figured out."

"Yeah, and it got him killed," Calvin said.

Mister Jordan stuck his head in the door. "Y'all better hurry on up, now. Them two bad uns could come back any time now."

Finder's Magic

"Naw, it's all right, Mister Jordan." I said. "Like you said before, they're pro'bly half-way to Macon by now. Besides, they don't stay here at night."

"What about that Jack?" Calvin asked. "We know he's still in town."

"Oh yeah, but I don't think he'd come back without Tugg, though. He don't even sneeze, 'less Tugg tells him it's alright."

Mister Jordan looked over his shoulder, then back to us, his forehead creased with worry. "Well now, I gots to get my Blue on home, 'fore nightfall. He be like me. We don't see too good after dark."

"You go ahead, Mister Jordan. Me and Calvin'll be fine."

"You sure 'bout that?"

"Yessir. We'll finish up our business here in a hurry.'

Mister Jordan left and I looked back at the book, studying the names and numbers with Calvin leaning over my shoulder.

Seconds later we heard Mister Jordan talking loud outside. "Evenin', boss. I got some good firewood for sale here. This be fine Georgia pine. It burn real hot."

Lord help us! Tugg and Jack had come back!

I looked around for a way out, my heart pounding. There was only one door--the one Tugg and Jack would be coming in, any second. I tried the window, but it was stuck. I couldn't get it open.

"Hide!" I whispered to Calvin.

Calvin pointed to a broom closet.

"You take it. It ain't big enough for the both of us. I'll find someplace else." I threw the book back in the box and snapped it shut. I dove under the desk in the knee hole, hugging the money box to my chest. The puppy scooted in with me. I didn't know whether to push him out, or hold him. He'd give me away, for sure.

Tugg slung the door open. "I thought you said you locked it." His big feet thumped on the wooden floor.

"I know I locked it." Jack shuffled in behind him. "Where's my little Dandy Lion?" He made kissy sounds. "Com'ere, Dandy.

Here boy." The pup whined and I pushed him out under the front of the desk. He went straight to Jack.

"There you are, you little rascal." I seen Jack's hands reach down and pick him up. "You bad boy. Did you make that puddle? Didja, huh?"

"Would you quite fawnin' over that stupid dog!" Tugg snapped. "You ain't got the smarts God give you. I distinctly remember telling' you to lock up. You can't be too careful with their kind hangin' around. Make sure the money box is where it's supposed to be."

I could see their legs from the knee hole of the desk. Tugg had a nerve hinting that Mister Jordan would steal from them. *They* was the thieves.

Jack said, "Dandy ain't no stupid dog." He ambled toward the wood box. I couldn't see the pup. Jack musta been carrying him.

Tugg moved away from the door. "Never mind. I'll do it myself." I heard wood from the box hit the floor. A piece slid under the desk and whacked my shin. I clamped my lips shut to keep from yelping.

"It ain't here!" he shouted.

Tugg busted out the door. Jack didn't go 'til after he put the pup back in his box. His long legs took him out the door in a couple of strides. They was going after Mister Jordan. I couldn't let them hurt that poor old man. They'd give him enough grief because of me. I shot out from under the desk, the box still in my hands. By the time I got to the door, they was already dragging Mister Jordan from his wagon.

I held up the box. "Hey, you two big dummies," I yelled. "You lookin' for this?"

Tugg's head jerked around. Jack stood there with his mouth open.

I leaped off the stoop and lit out for the train yard as fast as my legs would carry me. I felt pretty sure I could outrun Tugg, but I wasn't so sure about Jack. At least, there'd be hiding places in boxcars and such.

Finder's Magic

I hit the tracks, flat out, matching my strides with the crossties. My side started to burn, but I kept running. I knew I was a goner unless I got a good jump on Jack. That thought alone gave me another burst of speed.

I made it to the split in the tracks where they back the boxcars up to the dock to unload the big bales of cotton. Almost out of breath, I couldn't go much farther. I looked back. There wasn't no sign of Jack or Tugg. Why wasn't they chasing me? I couldn't figure it out.

It was only a few more steps to the dock. If I could just get into the mill before they caught up with me, someone there would help me. They had to. Tugg and Jack couldn't kill me with other folks about. *Could they?*

I rolled up on the dock, took another quick look over my shoulder. I stumbled to the door and grabbed the handle. It wouldn't budge. A trickle of sweat ran down the side of my face as I yanked on the door. How could I have been so ignorant? I had plum forgot it was past quitting time. Everything was locked up tighter'n granny's corset. I was as good as dead.

Chapter Sixteen

Sometimes Mister Murphy worked late. He might still be inside. I raised my fist to knock on the door, but something wrapped around my ankle. *A snake!* I commenced to stomping and kicking like a lunatic. In my fit, I stomped on a big gray cat's foot. We both yowled and squalled so loud you'd think we had been snake bit.

A woman opened the door a crack and peeped out, looking all wild-eyed an' scared. She must have been cleaning up the in the offices. I didn't wait to find out. I yanked the door open and flew past her, nearly bowling her over. She yelled for me to stop. I didn't slow down to hear what else she was hollering, but I could tell she was all riled up from the edge in her voice.

"I gotta see Mister Murphy," I yelled. It didn't matter what she said, my life depended on getting' to the mill owner. I zigzagged through the silent machinery. When I figured out she wasn't chasing me, I slowed down to a trot and tried to catch my breath.

Mister Murphy's office was dark. His door was locked. I was too late. He'd already gone home. *What was I gonna do now?* I sat down on a stack of newspapers by the door, with the box in my lap and my head in my hands.

Finder's Magic

All through the shadowy mill, rows of yarn streamed down to the spindles. Bits of fuzz dangled here and there. It made me think of a giant spider web, with me the helpless fly tangled up in it. There was no way out. No one to help me. I wanted my papa. Did he know what a mess I'd got myself into?

I'd never been in the mill when it was quiet like that before...dead quiet. There wasn't no use going back outside. The mill would be as good a hiding place as any, for the night at least. I crept down the wooden stairs to the opening room, where they busted open the big cotton bales to send up to the carders. Mountains of fluffy white cotton looked like great piles of summer clouds. Maybe that's what it looked like in heaven where Papa had gone. Still clutching Tugg and Jack's money box, I climbed up onto a busted bale. I lay down and cried like a baby... cried 'til I couldn't cry no more.

My head swam and I musta blacked out. When I come to, I lay real still, listening. A noise, so loud it rattled the rafters, almost made me jump outta my britches. A cold sweat popped out all over my body. Cotton stuck to the palms of my hands. Tugg's voice boomed through the stillness. "Hey, kid! Come on out. We know you're in here." He waited a second, then yelled, "Bring back the box and nobody gets hurt."

My hands trembled as I laid them on the money box beside me. For a heartbeat, I had a notion to give it back to them, but then I thought better of it. Soon as they got what they wanted, they'd kill me. So I crept over to one of the big tubes that sucked the cotton upstairs to the carding machines. I crawled way back into it where nobody would be able to see me, and prayed to God they didn't turn the machine on.

"You better get out here." Tugg yelled. "We got your little colored buddy with us."

Good Lord Almighty! That's why they didn't follow me. How could they have caught Calvin? He could outrun the whole lot of us.

"Don't do it, Hank! They means to kill us both!"

"You shut your face!" Tugg yelled. There was a loud smack,

flesh against flesh.

I flinched as if I'd been hit. Calvin didn't make no more noise. *Lordy! Had they killed him already?*

Tugg yelled, "We ain't gonna play hide'n-seek. We know you're in here. Come sunup tomorrow morning, we're gonna do us a little fishin' from the train trestle. We got us some good tender bait here. You better be there, with our money, or the fish is gonna be nibblin' on a little dark meat."

"Yeah," Jack hollered. "Don't get no ideas 'bout going to the law, neither. We got the sheriff in our hip pocket. You'll be the one endin' up in jail, right alongside that old colored man that helped you break in our office."

"Shut up, Jack!" Tugg growled.

Tugg and Jack had murdered my best friend while I hid and watched. Mister Jordan was locked up in jail...or worse. Now they had Calvin. It couldn't get much worse, not unless they got me too. My hand bumped the money box. The money was our only weapon. It was the only thing them two cared about. I had to think fast.

They might not have known for sure if I was still in the mill, even if the cleaning lady told them she'd seen me. Common sense told me if I just kept quiet, they'd go away. But then, I ain't never been strong on common sense. Besides, Calvin needed my help right then. No matter how scared I was, I had to find a way to save him. He'd risked his life to help me. How could I do any less for him?

My papa taught me if a bad dog was after you, run at him and make a lot of noise. The dog'll turn tail and run every time. I shoved the money box into the tube as far as I could reach. I was fixin' to make some noise.

Yelling at the top of my lungs, I shouted, "You better not hurt my friend, or I swear, you'll never see one nickel of that money." My voice bounced around the walls and echoed back at me. I prayed I sounded braver than I felt and that they couldn't tell where I was hiding.

"Don't you fret now, boy." Tugg tried to make his voice sound

Finder's Magic

kindly. "Nobody's gonna get hurt."

Kindly as a copperhead.

"Matter of fact," Tugg shouted, "why don't you just bring the box out here? We can settle this right here and now, man to man. Why, we'll even throw in a re-ward to show we mean no harm. How's that sound?"

Oh, sure. Reward me by bashing in my head and throwing me on the tracks. Tugg was baiting me. *I'm no fool.* The floor boards creaked above me. It had to be Jack, sneaking around, trying to find me. I held my breath and lay as still as I could, listening for Jack's footsteps.

Tugg hollered again. "What d'ya say, kid?" His voice sounded sweet as molasses. "Why don't you save us all a lot of trouble? Think what you could do with some extra money." He lowered his voice, but I could still hear him. He might as well have been right there in that tube beside me. "Any sign of him, Jack?"

"Naw," Jack said. "Forget it, Tugg. He could hide a million places in here. All these pipes and rafters make it dang-near impossible to tell where his voice came from."

"So this is the way it's gonna be, huh, kid?" All the sweetness was suddenly gone from his voice. "I'll give you one more chance. You got 'til dawn. Meet us at the train trestle with our money. If you ain't there, the darky is taking a long dive into a shallow river. An' you can be sure we'll track you down sooner or later."

They slammed the door when they left. That's got to be how a prison door sounds when it clangs shut. I was sure locked up with no way out.

The sounds in the old mill that night woulda scared a grown man. I'd never held much belief in haunts or ghosts, but the walls groaned and creaked like the rusty gate at the cemetery. Machinery clinked and snapped, cooling down as the night air seeped through the walls. Lint-covered floorboards sighed. It was hard to fathom how the quiet could be so loud. Just when I'd purt-near got used to all the creaking and groaning, the skittering noises started. *Rats!* Mercy, I hated rats!

Then if that wasn't enough, my eyes began to play tricks on me. I peeked over the edge of the bin and saw two big green eyes glowing back at me. The eyes blinked and turned away. A low growl set my teeth on edge. *Rats don't growl.* I felt around for some kind of weapon. My trembling hands touched the money box. I clutched it with both hands, ready to fling it at the green-eyed monster.

Silently, the critter sprung up to the window sill. I could see the dark shape of a cat, probably the one I'd stepped on outside. My racing heart gradually slowed. There was more skittering noises. The cat pounced. I heard squeaking--then quiet. *Good job, cat!* One rat down, about a million to go.

I had lots of time for thinking that night. There was no doubt in my mind that Tugg and Jack had been stealing from me, the other workers and from Mister Murphy. The names in the book was mostly kids who didn't have no grownups in their family working at the mill. I tried to think of someone who'd believe me and help us. I was afraid to go to the sheriff after what Jack said. If it was true, he'd side with them. Mister Murphy would most likely believe them, too. He'd think I was the thief and murderer. I knew Mama would believe me, but I didn't want to put her in danger, too.

Calvin's people had helped us, but now Mister Jordan's wife was dead and he was in jail. I was on my own. It was all up to me. I didn't think I was smart enough to do it alone, so I did a lot of praying. I thought about everyone I cared about, Papa, Mama, Jeb, Blaze--and now Calvin and Miz Mancala, too. Nothing could bring Papa or Jeb back. I even told the Lord it didn't matter if I never got to buy Blaze back, if he'd just help me save Calvin's life. I wanted to see my mama, too.

When I finally drifted off to sleep, I had a terrible nightmare. I dreamt I saw Calvin floating face-down in the river. A cold breeze riffled the muddy water. Then Miz Mancala come walking right out on the water, like Jesus in the Bible. She rolled Calvin over. But it wasn't him. It was me!

I heard a clanking sound. Miz Mancala pointed up. There,

Finder's Magic

under the train trestle, the hand trolley bobbed on its rusty cable.

I woke up shivering. What did the dream mean? What was Miz Mancala trying to tell me? I tried to use *my mind's eye* like she told me. My mind kept going back that long train trestle reaching out across the river, the bucket swaying below it, and the muddy river twenty foot below.

The bucket! Could we use it to get away from Tugg and Jack? I didn't know how I could get Calvin away from them, but I had to try. I still had their stolen money--the one thing them two cared about. They'd killed once because of it. They wouldn't blink an eye at killing me and Calvin to get it back.

Chapter Seventeen

I hurried to my work station to snag a few things I'd need. There wasn't no cause to worry about workers coming in. It was Sunday and the mill was shut down all day. I grabbed a piece of tarp, an oil can for the rusty pulley and a knife to cut the ropes if they had Calvin tied up. And finally, I picked up the stack of newspapers outside Mister Murphy's office.

The knife felt cold in my shaking hands as I cut the newspaper into strips. It was the same knife Jeb had used to dig splinters out of my bare feet last summer. The wooden floor was worn out from heavy bins rolling over it. Splinters in your feet was a part of working at the mill, same as lint in your nose, in your hair... everywhere. I wrapped the tools in the tarp. Looking down the aisle, I could almost picture Jeb standing at his station, grinning back at me with his cap cocked over to one side.

"I sure miss you Jeb," I whispered. "I won't never forget you. They ain't gonna get away with killin' you."

Outside, the air still had a chill to it, but not as much as before. A light misty rain fell. The sky looked like I felt, dark and weighted down. Gas lights lit up the underneath and rain filled the clouds like tears, threatening to let loose in a flood. I sucked it up. There wasn't no time for bawling.

Finder's Magic

It was still dark when I got to the bridge. I didn't show myself, for fear Tugg and Jack was out of sight someplace, watching. I hid the things I'd borrowed from the mill at the base of the bridge. The cable on the hand car clanked, just like in my dream.

I sucked in a deep breath, and then crept up to the bridge. Far below, the muddy river flowed silent as a grave. A couple of mud ducks bobbed on the ripples. I was light-headed and my legs felt so weak I didn't trust them. I dropped to my knees, stuffed the box in my shirt and crawled out onto the bridge. The metal box was ice cold against my ribs. The oily creosote on the ties burned my nose. It stained my hands and the knees of my pants rusty-brown. Midway across, I stood up and held on to the hand rail. *Breathe slow. Stay calm. Don't look down.*

I grabbed hold of a brace above my head and started climbing. The wind whistled around me. The wooden braces was wet and slippery. Splinters bit into my hands. My muddy shoes kept slipping. When I got about ten foot above the tracks, I locked one leg around a brace and held the money box in both hands. My hands shook so hard I was afraid I'd drop it in the river. I jammed it in tight between the braces, leaving it sticking out on the side where the hand trolley was.

I hadn't expected going down to be as hard as going up. It was harder, even without the box. I was as weak as a sickly kitten. I hadn't had nothing to eat since the crappies me and Calvin cooked the day before.

At the river's edge, I found some flat rocks and put them in my pocket. Five of 'em, just like David, in the Bible. Difference was, he only had one giant to face. Two was coming after me.

The wind had picked up, and the mist turned to a steady rain. I looked at the sky. The clouds had red streaks in the east. It reminded me of another of Mama's sayings--"Red sky in the morning, sailor take warning."

There was one more climb to make--up the ladder to the bucket. Then I remembered, too late, we'd left it on the other side of the river. My head jerked to the platform. I don't know how, but the bucket was there, right where I needed it. Maybe the good Lord was answering my prayers, after all. I took a few seconds to say thanks, and ask Him for a whole lot more help.

I grabbed my bundle of tools and scrambled up the ladder before I lost my nerve. The rain stung my face and blurred my eyes. When I put my stuff in the bucket, the borrowed knife slipped out of the rolled up tarp. It splashed in the river twenty foot below. Miz Mancala's words come back to me, "There is danger in a high place." For a few seconds, I couldn't catch my breath.

I sat down on the wooden platform and kicked the ladder loose. It crashed in pieces at the river's edge. No one could climb up after me, but I couldn't change my mind and climb down neither. No way out but on the other side. I oiled the pulley and cable over the bucket, so it would move easy and we could make a fast getaway. The red streaks in the sky faded to the color of a rotten peach. A bad storm was coming, sure as shootin'. A rooster crowed. The wind carried smells of biscuits baking and fatback frying from shanties across the river--all them good smells made me feel even worse.

I pulled the bucket out to the middle of the river. I hunkered down low in the bucket and pulled the tarp over me. The cold from the sides and bottom of the metal bucket seeped through my clothes, throbbing like a body-sized toothache.

When I heard 'em, coming, I peeked out from under the tarp, opening it just a little slit. They come from the north side of the bridge, half dragging Calvin. They had Calvin hobbled, the rope around both ankles and not enough slack to walk good, let alone run if he got the chance. He kind of shuffled along. Jack had a coil of rope slung over his shoulder. Tugg held a shorter rope, tied to Calvin's wrists. He gave it a jerk that made Calvin stumble.

I wondered how Calvin would be able to step across the ties on the open part of the bridge. He could slip and fall through the tracks. If he lived through the fall, he couldn't swim as he was hog-tied, like a pig for slaughter.

Finder's Magic

Jack hoisted him over his shoulder. Jack was strong, skinny as he was. He carried Calvin out to the middle of the bridge and stood him against the railing.

I swallowed hard. I might be seeing my papa sooner than I planned. I didn't have no idea what to do, now that they was there, right above me. Cowering under the heavy tarp, I started to sweat even in the cold.

Tugg's head swiveled back and forth. He didn't think to look down, but Jack looked over the rail. "Lookie there, Tugg. Some fool left that ol' bucket out here in the middle of the bridge."

Since the bucket set back under the bridge a bit, I didn't think he could see me, but I shrank behind the tarp, leaving only enough room for one eye to peep through. Lordy, how my heart pounded.

"Shut up, Jack!" Tugg whacked Jack's shoulder. "Watch for the kid."

Jack looked across the bridge. I willed Calvin to look down through the cross ties--and finally, he did. I pulled the tarp back enough for him to see my face. Calvin's eyes went big as saucers. When I put my finger to my lips, he nodded the least little bit. Then he stared across the river toward the shanties and Miz Mancala's cabin. I looked, too.

I swear on my papa's grave, there stood Miz Mancala, all shimmery and bright. I heard her drum beating softly. She held her arms wide, then scooped them to her chest, the way she had when she told me how I had the power of the whole world. I tried to remember what else she'd said.

How could I call on the power of the whole world?

"Together," she'd said. "Together, you are strong." Her pale eyes looked straight at me. She nodded. The drums went silent.

Tugg's voice shattered the quiet of the morning. "Get out here, McCord! Or else your buddy goes in the river." He turned to Jack. "Dangle him over the side."

Jack took the coil of rope from his shoulder. He tied it under Calvin's arms.

"No! Please, mister! Don't throw me over. I can't swim. He'll come. I know Hank will come."

"Stop your snivelin'." Tugg stuffed a rag in Calvin's mouth and tied it with his dirty bandanna. "That'll shut you up."

I just about gagged at the thought of that nasty bandanna in Calvin's mouth. I couldn't get my mind around what was happening.

How could I have been so crazy to think I could save Calvin from Tugg and Jack?

Jack said, "Why don't we give him a little more time, Tugg. Ain't no need to get in a hurry. I mean, who's the kid gonna go tell, anyway?"

"You ain't goin' soft on me, are ya, Little?" Tugg snarled. "You wanna swing for murder?"

"Naw, I was just thinkin'--"

"Well stop thinkin' and do what you're told," Tugg yelled.

Jack lowered Calvin over the rail. He had the rest of the rope coiled around his arm. Calvin dangled a couple of feet above the bucket, just out of my reach. But above was good. At least I wouldn't have to try to *lift* him into the bucket. Now if I could just figure out how to *reach* him and pull him in.

Calvin looked down at me. There was pure terror in his eyes. Tears glistened on his cheeks. I held onto the cable and pulled myself up, my feet on either side of the top of the bucket. Lordy, how my legs trembled. The bucket rocked. I was so scared, I thought I would pass out.

Calvin seemed to figure out what I was trying to do. He pumped his legs to make his body swing. He swung closer and closer.

Jack leaned way over the rail just as I caught hold of Calvin's legs and pulled him into the bucket. "Hey! Whatta ya think you're do--" His words ended in a scream as he slipped over the rail. He went kicking and screaming, the rope still wrapped around his arm.

I held onto Calvin with everything I had. Jack's weight almost jerked us both out of the bucket after him. Either our

Finder's Magic

weight together was heavier than Jack, or the rope come loose from him. The bucket threatened to jump off the cable though, the way it bounced and swung. I heard a loud bang. Sparks flew from the pulley. At first, I didn't know what the sound was. I thought the cable was breaking, but then something zinged past my head. I looked up. Tugg had a gun pointed at my head.

"I ain't got your money," I yelled.

"Where is it?" Tugg shouted. "Tell me now, or so help me, I'll put the next bullet right through your little white-trash head!"

I pointed to the box lodged in the braces. "Up there!"

Tugg looked up. It gave me a chance to get a rock out of my pocket. I threw as hard as I could, aiming for the box. My throw went off to one side. Tugg turned back around with his gun aimed at me again. My next throw was right on the money, so to speak. The rock hit the corner of the box and knocked it loose. It landed on a cross tie and flew open. The thin sheets of paper scattered in the wind. Tugg cursed and dove after the paper tossed about by the wind. He didn't even notice they was only cut-up pieces of newspaper.

The rumble started out low. The bucket trembled. The early morning freight train's whistle screamed a warning as its brakes screeched, metal against metal. As in answer to that screech, the rusty cable gave way. One of Tugg's shots must have weakened it. We hit the water hard. It was ice cold. I opened my mouth to scream, but the muddy river water filled my mouth and nose with a bitter rusty taste. It cut off my breath, paralyzed my body and numbed my brain.

It seemed like forever before my head come up outta the water. I yelled for Calvin. I couldn't see him nowhere. My cold hands wouldn't work right. I thrashed around and finally got a hold of the rope. I could still feel Calvin's weight against it. I dog-paddled toward the bank, as fast as I could, holding the rope. My arms and legs felt like they was full of lead. As soon as my feet touched bottom, I stood and pulled Calvin to me. He was limp as a dish rag. I locked my frozen arms around his chest and hauled him to the bank.

He wasn't moving. I jerked the rag from his mouth, rolled him over on his stomach and started pounding him on his back.

"Don't die, Calvin! Don't die," I cried over and over.

He began to cough and choke. He threw up muddy river water.

A couple of colored men run down from the back of the train. Porters, I figured. They wore fancy uniforms.

"What in Tarnation was you young uns doing up there?" one asked. "That ain't no place to play. Don't you know you could have been killed?"

They seen the ropes on Calvin's wrists and ankles. They both turned to me with hard looks on their faces.

One of them men asked, "What's going on here? Did you tie this boy up?"

My teeth chattered so hard, I couldn't answer. I shook my head. My head pounded. Calvin's lips had done turned blue and he was still throwing up muddy water. One of them took his coat off and wrapped it around Calvin. The other one helped me out of Papa's wet coat and shrugged his off and give it to me. "We gotta get you boys warmed up. We got blankets in the train." They picked Calvin up and carried him up to the caboose. I stumbled after them, best I could.

Another man trotted down from the front of the train, a shiny chain dangling from his hand. He asked, "Boy, did you know that big man up on the tracks?"

I nodded and crumbled to the ground. I ached all over and my legs was too weak to hold me up another second.

The man helped me up the hill to the back of the train. Someone tossed him a blanket and he wrapped around my shoulders. I sat down beside the tracks.

"I tried to warn him with the whistle," he said. "But he acted like he never even heard it. There weren't no way I could get stopped in time." He opened his hand and stared at what he was holding. His hand shook. Then he looked down at me. "Why was he up there?"

Finder's Magic

I opened my mouth to answer, but nothing come out.

"Here," the man said. "I think this belonged to him. Since you knew him, you can take it to his kin. "He dropped Tugg's fancy pocket watch into my hand, like he wanted rid of it. I sat there staring at the watch.

The crystal was shattered and the hands stopped at 6:35. The cover dangled by a tiny gold hinge. Inside was a picture of a man and a woman. The man's face looked a lot like Tugg, except he had dark hair. The woman had wavy, light colored hair. I turned it over with fingers still numb from the cold. There was some fancy writing on the back. It was scratched up and hard to read. *To my husband Theo Arnold, June 15th, 1872*. I wondered if it was Tugg's mama and papa. I thought about throwing it in the river, but something made me keep it. Maybe Tugg still had some kin somewhere. Even someone as mean as Tugg Arnold once had a mama and a papa who cared about him.

More folks had got off the train and gathered around. They stared at me as if I was a side show at the circus. There was a big commotion around the train's engine on the bridge. Steam hissed down through the timbers.

Men had lined up and down the river bank with long poles. Bits of paper still drifted down. Some of it floated in the middle of the river. One man waded out into the river and picked up a piece. "It's just newspaper!" he shouted.

I thought of what Mama would say. "The love of money is the root of evil." I agreed with her. Just look where it'd got Tugg and Jack.

Mama also says bad things happen in threes.

Someone hollered from across the river. "Hey, we got the other one. He's dead, too. Neck's broke."

I could see the shock of dark hair hanging down on his forehead as they pulled him from the water. It was Jack. First it was my friend, Jeb, now Tugg and Jack. That made three, unless you counted Missus Jordan, but Miz Mancala had said she wasn't gonna live much longer, anyway.

"Where's Calvin," I asked one of the men. "Is he alright?" They helped me inside the caboose where Calvin was bundled up in blankets, sitting next to a little stove.

Calvin's eyes met mine. He still looked in bad shape. He reached his hand out. I grabbed it and held on tight. It was cold as ice, but strong.

Together we was strong.

Finder's Magic

Chapter Eighteen

Sunday, December 31, 1911

It was New Year's Eve and the next day would be my birthday. Just a week before, I didn't think I would live to see it. The clouds broke, leaving the sky such a bright blue it made my eyes water. Mama'd let me sleep late while she went to church. She wouldn't hear of me going back to work for a full week after we took that dunking in the river.

Calvin caught a bad cold, but he was getting better under Miz Mancala's nursing. Mama even went to check on him a couple of times. I was real proud of her for that. I never even got the sniffles.

Mister Murphy 'bout popped a gut when I told him about Tugg and Jack stealing from him and us workers. I don't think he really believed me until I showed him where I'd hid the money and the extra payroll book in the mill. After reading Tugg's book, Mister Murphy made good on all the wages they'd stole. He went and got Mister Jordan out of jail. Then he give me fifty dollars reward. It'd take me forever to earn that kind of money working at the mill. He never gave Calvin nothing.

Mama got three days off with pay to take care of me, not that I needed taking care of. I still hadn't told nobody about the money I took from Jack. I knew it wasn't right to keep it, but I couldn't figure out what to do with it. I'd promised half of it to Calvin. I figured the mill owed it to him. It was still hid in our hollow tree.

Tugg's broken pocket watch lay on the window sill. I picked it up and rubbed my fingers over the shiny case, then opened it and looked at the pictures inside. I didn't know if Tugg's mama and papa was still alive or not. If they was, I'd take the watch to them some day.

Neighbors had carried in so much food, you'd think somebody died. There was even a basket of fresh vegetables from someone's winter garden. Mama made a carrot pie that was even better'n sweet potato pie. I ate so much of it Mama fussed that I was gonna make myself sick. Everyone made out like I was some kind of hero. I told 'em Jeb was the hero. He caught onto Tugg and Jack's scheme first, but it took both me and Calvin, together, to stop 'em.

I was restless and needed to stretch my legs. I put on Papa's coat. Mama had washed and dried it, and took it in to fit me. I laid Tugg's watch back on the window sill and stuck a couple of carrots in my pocket. Mama'd helped me pick out a nice teapot from the mercantile. It weren't near as fancy as the one Miz Mancala had before, but it was the best I could do. Mama wrapped it up in a dishtowel so it wouldn't get broke. I tucked it under my arm and stepped out into the sunshine. The warmth felt good on my face. I was glad for the warm spell after all the cold weather.

I headed straight to Miz Mancala's cabin. Calvin and Miz Mancala was setting out on the porch, talking to Mister Jordan. Calvin and Mister Jordan waved when they seen me walking up the path. Jack's little cream-colored puppy lay on the porch between them. He stood up and commenced wiggling soon as he seen me.

"Mornin' Miz Mancala," I said. "I brung you another teapot

to replace the one me and Calvin busted." I unwrapped it and laid it in her lap. "It ain't near as fancy as the one you had, but it's the best I could get from the company store."

Miz Mancala ran her hands over the pot. "Thank you, Hank. It's lovely."

I plopped down on the porch beside Calvin. The pup waddled over and stood against my chest. He licked my face. His puppy-breath was wet and smelled like cooked rutabagas. "You give him a name yet?" I tried to dodge the pup's quick tongue.

Calvin laughed, but started coughing. When he finally stopped coughing, he said, "I decided not to change his name. I heard Jack call him 'Dandy.' It suits him." Calvin grinned. "Miz Mancala's cat don't like him none too good."

Miz Mancala chuckled.

"I'll bet he don't," I said. Remembering what Miz Mancala'd said about her "slave name," I said. "Sometimes a name's all a body's got. Hey," I said, changing the subject. "Y'all need any food? Me and Mama got way more'n we can eat, just the two of us."

"Naw, ever'body been bringin' so much food, me an' Miz Mancala can't eat it all up, neither. Miz Lizbeth brung some of her 'lasses cookies." He nodded toward a basket. "Help y'self," he said.

"Thanks," I said, popping one in my mouth. It took me back to when me and Calvin first come to Miz Mancala's.

"I got me a job," Calvin said.

Mister Jordan leaned forward. "Soon as he able. We ain't gonna rush it none."

Calvin waved him off. "I'll be fine in no time. Just got this little ol' cough to get rid of."

I looked from him to Mister Jordan. "Well, what's this job?" I asked.

They looked at each other. Mister Jordan said, "I's getting' too old to haul the wood all the time. I needs me a partner. Po' ol' Blue's might nigh as wore-down as me. He need a partner, too."

Calvin sat there watching me. I said, "So, is that it? You gonna be Mister Jordan's partner?"

Calvin nodded. "Soon as I can buy a mule, so Blue don't have to do all the haulin'," he said. "It's gonna take me some time to save up enough money to do that."

Then I knew why I hadn't told nobody about the money we got from Jack. Calvin's daddy had been lynched by white men. Then he saved me and purt-near drowned because of it. Mister Murphy never give him a dime. That money was rightfully Calvin's. "We got more'n enough money for you to buy a good mule. They may even be enough to get another wagon, too."

"Nossir! I ain't touchin' that money," Calvin said, his jaw set all stubborn-like.

Mister Jordan stood up. "I reckon I'll be goin'. Blue's for sure wonderin' where I be."

Me and Calvin stood up, too. "Mister Jordan," I said. "I never really thanked you proper for all you done for me and Calvin."

I threw my arms around him and hugged him. He patted my back, kind of shy. When I let go of him, he wiped the corner of his eye. "You boys take care," he said. He nodded to Miz Mancala. "Afternoon, ma'am," he said, then socked his hat on his head and walked away.

Miz Mancala rose from her chair. "I believe I'll go inside. You lads stay and visit as long as you like."

The door thumped behind her. I spun around to face Calvin again. "I can't believe you'd be so bullheaded. You got to think about somebody sides your own stubborn self. You know you owe Miz Mancala, after she took you in like she did. This ain't no way for her to live." I seen a shadow of doubt cross Calvin's face. I was getting to him. "And what about poor old Mister Jordan? Haulin' all that wood's killin' him. You owe it to 'em both to take that money and help 'em out."

Calvin stared at his feet. "I never thought if it that way. You right. I owe them a lot." He looked up at me suddenly. "That reminds me. I told Miz Mancala 'bout the dream I had."

"What dream?" I asked, setting back down on the porch and

reaching for another cookie.

"You remember, I told you about it," he said, sounding put-out. "The one where I was pinned down in a ditch an' you charged up on a big red horse, an' saved me."

"Oh, that dream," I lied. I didn't remember it.

"Yeah, she say maybe it was God tryin' to tell me something. I think I was supposed to save you, but you went and saved me. Now, you giving me all that money. I ain't never gonna reach my higher plane."

I grinned. "Shoot! The way I figure it, we're about even on that score."

Calvin reached down and picked the puppy up. "They's something else." He took a deep breath, rubbing the pup's head. "You asked me if I'd ever done something I was ashamed of."

"I remember," I said.

"Well there was--is. It's about my mama. I let you think she died when I was a baby." He cleared his throat. "Well, that ain't the truth. She run off and left me and Daddy to go work in a dance hall. She didn't care about us. She's... She's like that lady we seen with Jack outside the beer joint."

"Calvin, I don't know why your mama left you and your daddy, but there wasn't nothing you could'a done about it. You wasn't more'n a baby then. It weren't your fault. You just put that outta your head, 'cause you didn't have nothin' to do with it." I took a bite of cookie. "Um, speakin' of things we didn't have nothing to do with. That morning under the trestle, the bucket shoulda been on the other side of the bridge, where we'd left it. But it was on the mill side, right where I needed it. It was a miracle."

Calvin grinned. "I can explain that. The night when we split up after seeing Jack, I used it to cross the river, and then I put it back. I thought you might need it. I was sure right about that."

"Zowie! Were you ever! I didn't know you could move it across without being in it." Then I heard Miz Mancala's drum beating softly from inside the cabin. "It always gives me the creeps when she starts playin' that ol' drum."

Finder's Magic

"What you mean?" Calvin asked. "Miz Mancala don't play the drum. It belonged to her husband. He died a long time ago."

"Don't you hear it?" I asked.

Calvin looked at me like I'd lost my mind. He shook his head, not taking his eyes off me, but then I seen a flicker in his eyes. He was messing with me, as usual.

Or was he?

I stood and brushed the cookie crumbs from my lap. "I got to go say hey to another friend. I patted the carrots in my pocket. "Then I got to get on home."

Calvin grinned. "You ain't foolin' nobody. You're gonna go see that horse. You an' horses."

"Yup. See ya." I waved my hand. I had a spring in my step as I walked away. I'd finally put one over on Calvin Yates, getting him to take the money. It felt right good.

"See ya," Calvin called out.

I cut across to the livery stable. In the stall out back, the big sorrel lifted his head and nickered when he seen me. I stepped up on the fence rail and whistled. He pranced around, tossing his head and holding his tail high. He looked a mess--dirty and matted.

"Playin' hard to get, are ya?" I dangled a carrot over the rail.

Watching me from the far side, he shook his head and snorted.

"You know you want it," I teased, giving the carrot a shake.

He took a step toward me, reaching his nose out, his nostrils flared. He was muddy and his mane was one tangled knot.

"Still don't trust no one, do ya, big fella? Can't say as I blame you." I climbed up and threw my leg over the top rail, determined to wait as long as it took. "You gonna just stand over there and wish for this nice sweet carrot, or you gonna come over here and get it?"

He seemed to make up his mind finally...and inched closer. I could tell he wanted the carrot real bad, but he wasn't ready to let down his guard all the way. I sat still, holding the carrot

Finder's Magic

out to him. When he took the carrot, he didn't bolt away, like I expected him to. I reached my hand out slow and rubbed his neck. He took another step forward and nudged me hard with his head. I had to grab his neck to keep from tumbling over backwards.

Leaning against him, I soaked up his warmth, felt the slow steady thump of his heart, my heart matching his, beat for beat.

"Well I'll swan," a deep voice said, behind me.

The big red horse tensed and raised his head, his ears backed. I turned around to see the man who ran the stable. "I wasn't hurtin' nothin', mister," I said quick-like.

The man chuckled. "I can see that. Nobody's been able to touch that horse for at least a week. That's why he looks the way he does. I was gonna clean him up and sell him for his feed bill, but I can't get near him. He's a skittish devil. Used to a real rough hand."

"He's for sale?" I asked, my heard doing flip-flops inside my chest. "How much?" I thought about my "deal" with God not to try to get Blaze back, but this wasn't Blaze.

"Hold on now, son. This stallion's way too much horse for a youngun. Like I said, he's used to a heavy hand."

"Heavy hand" was a nice way of saying how Tugg mistreated him. "I can handle him, mister. How much?" The stallion nudged me again. He didn't want me to stop petting him. I scratched his ears, and his eyelids drooped. He lowered his head so I could reach higher on his neck.

"Maybe you could son, or maybe not but then there's the matter of where you'd keep him. You gotta have a strong corral for a stallion. You got a place?"

My hopes sank like a rock in the river. "Nossir, I work at the mill. Me an' Mama live in one of the cabins."

The man stepped up to the fence. The horse's eyes opened, and I could feel his neck muscles knot up again. "Easy, boy, easy. Nobody's gonna hurt you," I said stroking his powerful neck.

126

The livery man said, "What's your name, son?"

"Henry McCord, sir, but my friends call me Hank."

"Hank McCord?" His eyebrows shot up. "Ain't you the kid who caught Tugg an' his partner stealin' from the mill kids?" He stuck out his hand. "I'd like to shake your hand. That was a mighty brave thing you done."

"Nossir, it weren't brave. I was 'bout scared to death. I just didn't have no other choice. My friend Calvin Yates almost died."

He looked me up and down. Calvin Yates? He that Negro boy?"

I didn't like the way he said it, like it left a bad taste in his mouth. "He's my friend. He saved my life," I answered, not even bothering to say "sir," like Mama'd taught me.

"How old are you?" he asked. "I heard you was twelve, that right?"

"Yessir, I turn twelve tomorrow. It's my birthday." I wondered why he kept asking me all them questions.

"Well, you ain't got much muscles on you," he said, sizing me up. "But then, it don't really take muscles to handle a horse. Truth be known, it takes horse sense. You seem to have a way with horses. An' once in a blue moon, a one-man horse comes along. This one seems to have taken a shine to you."

I was scared to get my hopes up at the way this talk was going. "My papa always said I had a natural way with horses. He was real good with 'em. Mama says I take after him."

The livery man spit on the ground and kicked dirt over it. "Tugg Arnold owed me better'n fifty dollars when he went and got hisself killed by that train." He cocked his head to the side. "You got fifty dollars?"

"Yes sir!" I squared up my shoulders. "Mister Murphy give me a reward."

"All right, then. Fifty dollars and you can help out around here for his keep. You up for that?"

"You bet!" I said, grinning from ear to ear.

"I'll even throw in a saddle and bridle. But you got to show

Finder's Magic

up for work every morning." He stuck out his hand again.

"It's a deal!" I grabbed his big hand. I'd have to clear it with Mama, but I knew she'd say yes. I was so happy, I was about to bust. This was gonna be my best birthday ever.

On the way home, I thought about everything that'd happened. I missed Papa and Jeb something awful, but nothing could bring them back.

As I walked away, I heard the raspy cry of a red-tailed hawk and looked up. She soared in big lazy circles high above the trees. Papa loved red-tailed hawks. He said they was the farmer's friend 'cause they killed vermin. Standing there watching the hawk circle, I thought how much my life had changed, but yet some things go on the same. I'd always miss Papa and Jeb, but I'd hold onto them in my memories.

The hawk tucked her wings and dove behind the trees. She weren't gone forever, only out of sight, like Papa and Jeb. I'd see them again one day.

Walking along the river bank, I remembered seeing Miz Mancala on the other side, just before me and Calvin went in the river. *Had she really been there, or did I dream it?* I thought about everything she'd said, and I knew she was right about all of it. Miz Mancala's magic was her wisdom. Together, we was strong. That's the only way we'd reach our higher plane. In my mind's eye, I saw Miz Mancala smile... and it weren't spooky.